# MANALIVE

GILBERT K. CHESTERTON

# MANALIVE

# MANALIVE

BY
G. K. CHESTERTON

NEW YORK
JOHN LANE COMPANY
MCMXII

# CONTENTS

## PART I
## THE ENIGMAS OF INNOCENT SMITH

| CHAPTER | | PAGE |
|---|---|---|
| I | How the Great Wind Came to Beacon House | 1 |
| II | The Luggage of an Optimist | 26 |
| III | The Banner of Beacon | 48 |
| IV | The Garden of the God | 71 |
| V | The Allegorical Practical Joker | 95 |

## PART II
## THE EXPLANATIONS OF INNOCENT SMITH

| I | The Eye of Death; or, The Murder Charge | 137 |
|---|---|---|
| II | The Two Curates; or, The Burglary Charge | 184 |
| III | The Round Road; or, The Desertion Charge | 235 |
| IV | The Wild Weddings; or, The Polygamy Charge | 275 |
| V | How the Great Wind Went from Beacon House | 305 |

# MANALIVE

# PART I

# THE ENIGMAS OF INNOCENT SMITH

## CHAPTER I

## HOW THE GREAT WIND CAME TO BEACON HOUSE

A WIND sprang high in the west like a wave of unreasonable happiness and tore eastward across England, trailing with it the frosty scent of forests and the cold intoxication of the sea. In a million holes and corners it refreshed a man like a flagon, and astonished him like a blow. In the inmost chambers of intricate and embowered houses it woke like a domestic explosion, littering the floor with some professor's papers till they seemed as precious as fugitive, or blowing out the candle by which a boy read "Treasure Island" and wrapping him in roaring dark. But everywhere it bore drama into undra-matic lives, and carried the trump of crisis across the world. Many a harassed mother in a mean backyard had looked at five dwarfish shirts on the clothes-line as at some small, sick tragedy; it was as if she had hanged her five children. The wind came and they were full and kicking as if five fat imps had sprung into them; and far down in her oppressed subconsciousness she half remembered those coarse comedies of her fathers when the elves still dwelt in the homes of men. Many an unnoticed girl in a dank, walled garden had tossed herself into the hammock with the same intolerant gesture with which she might have tossed herself into the Thames; and that wind rent the waving wall of woods and lifted the hammock like a balloon, and showed her shapes of quaint cloud far beyond, and pictures of bright villages far below, as if she rode heaven in a fairy boat. Many a dusty clerk or curate plodding a telescopic road of poplar3 thought for the hundredth time that they were like the plumes of a hearse, when this invisible energy caught and swung and clashed them round his head like a wreath or salutation of seraphic wings. There was in it something more inspired and authoritative even than the old wind of the proverb; for this was the good wind that blows nobody harm.

The flying blast struck London just where it scales the northern heights, terrace above terrace, as precipitous as Edinburgh. It was round about this place that some poet, probably drunk, looked up astonished at all those streets gone skywards, and (thinking vaguely of glaciers and roped mountaineers) gave it the name of Swiss Cottage, which it has never been able to shake off. At some stage of those heights a terrace of tall gray houses, mostly empty and almost as desolate as the Grampians, curved round at the western end, so that the last building, a boarding establishment called "Beacon House," offered abruptly to the sunset its high, narrow, and towering termination, like the prow of some deserted ship.

The ship, however, was not wholly deserted. The proprietor of the boarding-house, a Mrs. Duke, was one of those helpless persons upon whom fate wars in vain; she smiled vaguely both before and after all her calamities; she was too soft to be hurt. But by the aid (or rather under the orders) of a strenuous niece she always kept the remains of a clientele, mostly of young but listless folks. And there were actually five inmates standing disconsolately about the garden when the great gale broke at the base of the terminal tower behind them, as the sea bursts against the base of an outstanding cliff.

All day that hill of houses over London had been domed and sealed up with cold cloud. Yet three men and two girls had at last found even the gray and chilly garden more tolerable than the black and cheerless interior. When the wind came it split the sky and shouldered the cloudland left and right; unbarring great clear furnaces of rolling gold. The burst of light released and the burst of air blowing seemed to come almost simultaneously; and the wind especially caught everything in a throttling violence. The bright short grass lay all one way like brushed hair. Every shrub in the garden tugged at its roots like a dog at the collar, and strained every leaping leaf after the hunting and exterminating element. Now and again a twig would snap and fly like a bolt from an arbalest. The three men stood stiffly and aslant against the wind, as if leaning against a wall. The two ladies disappeared into the house. Rather, to speak truly, they were blown into the house. Their two frocks, blue and white, looked like two big broken flowers, driving and drifting upon the gale. Nor is such a poetic fancy inappropriate, for there was something oddly romantic about this inrush of air and light after a long, leaden, and un-lifting day. Grass and garden trees seemed glittering with something at once good and unnatural like a fire from fairyland. It seemed like a strange sunrise at the wrong end of the day.

The girl in white dived in quickly enough, for she wore a white hat of the proportions of a parachute, which might have wafted her away into the coloured clouds of evening. She was their one splash of splendour and irradiated wealth in that impecunious place (staying there temporarily with a friend), an heiress in a small way, by name Rosamund Hunt, brown eyed, round faced, but resolute and rather boisterous. On top of her wealth she was good-humoured and rather good-looking; but she had not married, perhaps because there was always a crowd of men round her. She was not fast (though some might have called her vulgar), but she gave irresolute youths an impression of being at once popular and inaccessible. A man felt as if he had fallen in love with Cleopatra, or as if he were asking for a great actress at the stage door. Indeed, some theatrical spangles seemed to cling about Miss Hunt; she played the guitar and the mandoline; she always wanted charades; and with that great rending of the sky by sun and storm, she felt a girlish melodrama swell again within her. To the crashing orchestration of the air, the clouds rose like the curtain of some long expected pantomime.

Nor, oddly enough, was the girl in blue entirely unimpressed by this apocalypse in a private garden; though she was one of the most prosaic and practical creatures alive, she was indeed no other than the strenuous niece whose strength alone upheld that mansion of decay. But as the gale swung and swelled the blue and white skirts till they took on the monstrous mushroom contours of Victorian crinolines, a sunken memory stirred in her that was almost romance; a memory of a dusty volume of "Punch" in an aunt's house in infancy; pictures of crinoline hoops and croquet hoops and some pretty story, of which perhaps they were a part. This half-perceptible fragrance in her thoughts faded almost instantly, and Diana Duke entered the house even more promptly than her companion. Tall, slim, aquiline, and dark, she seemed made for such swiftness. In body she was of the breed of those birds and beasts that are at once long and alert, like greyhounds or herons or even like an innocent snake. The whole house revolved on her as on a rod of steel. It would be wrong to say that she commanded; for her own efficiency was so impatient that she obeyed herself before any one else obeyed her. Before electricians could mend a bell or locksmiths open a door, before dentists could pluck a loose tooth, or butlers draw a tight cork, it was done already with the silent vio-

lence of her slim hands. She was light; but there was nothing leaping about her lightness. She spurned the ground; and she meant to spurn it. People talk of the pathos and failure of plain women; but it is a more terrible thing that a beautiful woman may succeed in everything but womanhood.

"It's enough to blow your head off," said the young woman in white, going to the looking-glass.

The young woman in blue made no reply, but put away her gardening gloves, and then went to the sideboard and began to spread out an afternoon cloth for tea.

"Enough to blow your head off I say," said Miss Rosamund Hunt, with the unruffled cheeriness of one whose songs and speeches had always been safe for an encore.

"Only your hat, I think," said Diana Duke; "but I dare say that is sometimes more important."

Rosamund's face showed for an instant the offence of a spoilt child, and then the humour of a very healthy person. She broke into a laugh and said, "Well, it would have to be a big wind to blow your head off."

There was another silence; and the sunset breaking more and more from the sundering clouds, filled the room with soft fire and painted the dull walls with ruby and gold.

"Somebody once told me," said Rosamund Hunt, "that it's easier to keep one's head when one has lost one's heart."

"Oh, don't talk about such rubbish," said Diana with savage sharpness.

Outside, the garden was clad in a golden splendour; but the wind was still stiffly blowing, and the three men who stood their ground might also have considered the problem of hats and heads. And, indeed, their position, touching hats, was somewhat typical of them. The tallest of the three abode the blast in a high silk hat, which the wind seemed to charge as vainly as that other sullen tower, the house behind him. The second man tried to hold on a stiff straw hat at all angles, and ultimately held it in his hand. The third had no hat, and, by his attitude, seemed never to have had one in his life. Perhaps this wind was a kind of fairy wand to test men and women, for there was much of the three men in this difference.

The man in the solid silk hat was the embodiment of silkiness and solidity. He was a big, bland, bored, and (as some said) boring man, with flat fair hair and handsome heavy features; a prosperous young doctor by the name of Warner. But if his blondness and blandness seemed at first a little fatuous, it is certain that he was no fool. If Rosamund Hunt was the only person there with much money, he was the only person who had as yet found any kind of fame. His treatise on "The Probable Existence of Pain in the Lowest Organisms" had been universally hailed by the scientific world as at once solid and daring. In short, he undoubtedly had brains; and perhaps it was not his fault if they were the kind of brains that most men desire to analyze with a poker.

The young man who put his hat off and on was a scientific amateur in a small way, and worshipped the great Warner with a solemn freshness. It was in fact at his invitation that the distinguished doctor was present; for Warner lived in no such ramshackle lodging-house, but in a professional palace in Harley Street. This young man was really the youngest and best looking of the three. But he was one of those persons, both male and female, who seem doomed to be good-looking and insignificant. Brown haired, high coloured, and shy, he seemed to lose the delicacy of his features in a sort of blur of brown and red as he stood blushing and blinking against the wind. He was one of those obvious un-noticeable people: every one knew that he was Arthur Inglewood, unmarried, moral, decidedly intelligent, living on a little money of his own, and hiding himself in the two hobbies of photography and cycling. Everybody knew him and forgot him; even as he stood there in the glare of golden sunset there was something about him indistinct, like one of his own red-brown amateur photographs.

The third man had no hat; he was lean, in light, vaguely sporting clothes, and the large pipe in his mouth made him look all the leaner. He had a long ironical face, blue-black hair, the blue eyes of an Irishman, and the blue chin of an actor. An Irishman he was, an actor he was not, except in the old days of Miss Hunt's charades, being, as a matter of fact, an obscure and flippant journalist named Michael Moon. He had once been hazily supposed to be reading for the Bar; but (as Warner would say with his rather elephantine wit) it was mostly at another kind of bar that his friends found him. Moon, however, did not drink, nor even frequently get drunk, he simply was a gentleman who liked low company. This was partly because company is quieter than society, and if he enjoyed talking to a barmaid (as apparently he did), it was chiefly because the barmaid did the talking. Moreover he would often bring other talent to assist her. He shared that strange trick of all men of his type, intellectual and without ambition, the trick of going about with his mental inferiors. There was a small resident Jew named Moses Gould in the same boarding-house, a little man whose negro vitality and vulgarity amused Michael so much that he went round with him from bar to bar, like the owner of a performing monkey.

The colossal clearance which the wind had made of that cloudy sky grew clearer and clearer; chamber within chamber seemed to open in heaven. One felt one might at last find something lighter than light. In the fullness of this silent effulgence all things collected their colours again, the gray trunks turned silver and the drab gravel gold. One bird fluttered like a loosened leaf from one tree to another, and his brown feathers were brushed with fire.

"Inglewood," said Michael Moon, with his blue eye on the bird, "have you any friends?"

Doctor Warner mistook the person addressed, and turning a broad beaming face, said,—

"Oh, yes, I go out a great deal."

Michael Moon gave a tragic grin, and waited for his real informant, who spoke a moment after in a voice curiously cool, fresh and young, as coming out of that brown and even dusty exterior.

"Really," answered Inglewood, "I'm afraid I've lost touch with my old friends. The greatest friend I ever had was at school, a fellow named Smith. It's odd you should mention it, because I was thinking of him to-day, though I haven't seen him for seven or eight years. He was on the science side with me at school, a clever fellow though queer, and he went up to Oxford when I went to Germany. The fact is, it's rather a sad story. I often asked him to come and see me, and when I heard nothing I made inquiries you know. I was shocked to learn that poor Smith had gone off his head. The accounts were a bit cloudy of course. Some saying he had recovered again, but they always say that. About a year ago I got a telegram from him myself. The telegram, I'm sorry to say, put the matter beyond a doubt."

"Quite so," assented Dr. Warner stolidly; "insanity is generally incurable."

"So is sanity," said the Irishman, and studied him with a dreary eye.

"Symptoms?" asked the doctor. "What was this telegram?"

"It's a shame to joke about such things," said Inglewood, in his honest, embarrassed way; "the telegram was Smith's illness, not Smith. The actual words were, 'Man found alive with two legs.' "

"Alive with two legs," repeated Michael, frowning. "Perhaps a version of alive and kicking? I don't know much about people out of their senses; but I suppose they ought to be kicking."

"And people in their senses?" asked Warner, smiling.

"Oh, they ought to be kicked," said Michael with sudden heartiness.

"The message is clearly insane," continued the impenetrable Warner. "The best test is a reference to the undeveloped normal type. Even a baby does not expect to find a man with three legs."

"Three legs," said Michael Moon, "would be very convenient in this wind."

A fresh eruption of the atmosphere had indeed almost thrown them off their balance and broken the blackened trees in the garden. Beyond, all sorts of accidental objects could be seen scouring the wind-scoured sky, straws, sticks, rags, papers, and, in the distance, a disappearing hat. Its disappearance, however, was not final; after an interval of minutes they saw it again, much larger and closer, a white panama, towering up into the heavens like a balloon, staggering to and fro for an instant like a stricken kite, and then settling in the centre of their own lawn as falteringly as a fallen leaf.

"Somebody's lost a good hat," said Doctor Warner shortly.

Almost as he spoke, another object came over the garden wall, flying after the fluttering panama. It was a big green umbrella. After that came hurtling a huge yellow Gladstone bag, and after that came a figure like a flying wheel of legs, as in the shield of the Isle of Man.

But though for a flash it seemed to have five or six legs, it alighted upon two, like the man in the queer telegram. It took the form of a large light-haired man in gay green holiday clothes. He had bright blonde hair that the wind brushed back like a German's, a flushed eager face like a cherub's and a prominent pointing nose, a little like a dog's. His head, however, was by no means cherubic in the sense of being without a body. On the contrary, on his vast shoulders and shape, generally gigantesque, his head looked oddly and unnaturally small. This gave rise to a scientific theory (which his conduct fully supported) that he was an idiot.

Inglewood had a politeness instinctive and yet awkward. His life was full of arrested half gestures of assistance. And even this prodigy of a big man in green, leaping the wall like a bright green grasshopper, did not paralyze that small altruism of his habits in such a matter as a lost hat. He was stepping forward to recover the green gentleman's headgear, when he was struck rigid with a roar like a bull's.

"Unsportsmanlike!" bellowed the big man. "Give it fair play, give it fair play!" And he came after his own hat quickly, but cautiously, with burning eyes. The hat had seemed at first to droop and dawdle as in ostentatious languor on the sunny lawn; but the wind again freshening and rising it went dancing down the garden with the devilry of a pas-de-quatre. The eccentric went bounding after it with kangaroo leaps and bursts of breathless speech, of which it was not always easy to pick up the thread: "Fair play, fair play . . . sport of kings . . . chase their crowns . . . quite humane . . . tramontana . . . cardinal chase red hats . . . old English hunting . . . started a hat in Bramber Combe . . . hat at bay . . . mangled hounds. . . . Got him!"

As the wind rose out of a roar into a shriek, he leapt into the sky on his strong, fantastic legs, snatched at the vanishing hat, missed it, and pitched sprawling face foremost on the grass. The hat rose over him like a bird in triumph; but its triumph was premature. For the lunatic, flung forward on his hands, threw up his boots behind, waved his two legs in the air like symbolic ensigns (so that they thought again of the telegram), and actually caught the hat with his feet. A prolonged and piercing yell of wind split the welkin from end to end. The eyes of all the men were blinded by the invisible blast, as by a strange, clear cataract of transparency rushing between them and all objects about them. But as the large man fell back in a sitting posture, and solemnly crowned himself with the hat, Michael found, to his incredulous surprise, that he had been holding his breath like a man watching a duel.

While that tall wind was at the top of its sky-scraping energy, another short cry was heard, beginning very querulous, but ending very quick, swallowed in abrupt silence. The shiny black cylinder of Dr. Warner's official hat sailed off his head in the long, smooth parabola of an airship, and in almost cresting a garden tree was caught in the topmost branches. Another hat was gone. Those in that garden felt themselves caught in an unaccustomed eddy of things happening; no one seemed to know what would blow away next. Before they could speculate, the cheering and hallooing hat-hunter was already half way up the tree, swinging himself from fork to fork with his strong, bent, grasshopper legs, and still giving forth his gasping, mysterious comments.

"Tree of life . . . Tydrasil . . . climb for centuries perhaps . . . owls nesting in the hat . . . remotest generations of owls . . . still usurpers . . . gone to heaven . . . man in the moon wears it . . . brigand . . . not yours . . . belongs to depressed medical man ... in garden . . . give it up . . . give it up!"

The tree swung and swept and thrashed to and fro in the thundering wind like a thistle, and flamed in the full sunshine like a bonfire. The green, fantastic human figure, vivid against its autumn red and gold, was already among its highest and craziest branches, which by bare luck did not break with the weight of his big body. He was up there among the last tossing leaves and the first twinkling stars of evening, still talking to himself cheerfully, reasoningly, half apologetically, in little gasps. He might well be out of breath, for his whole preposterous raid had gone with one rush; he had bounded once the wall like a football, swept down the garden like a slide, and shot up the tree like a rocket. The other three men seemed buried under incident piled on incident, a wild world where one thing began before another thing left off. All three had the first thought. The tree had been there for the five years they had known the boarding-house. Each one of them was active and strong. No one of them had even thought of climbing it. Beyond that, Inglewood felt first the mere fact of colour. The bright brisk leaves, the bleak blue sky, the wild green arms and legs, reminded him irrationally of something glowing in his infancy; something akin to a gaudy man on a golden tree; perhaps it was only a painted monkey on a stick. Oddly enough, Michael Moon, though more of a humorist, was touched on a tenderer nerve, half remembered the old, young theatricals with Rosamund, and was amused to find himself almost quoting Shakespeare—

"For valour is not love, a Hercules Still climbing trees in the Hesperides."

Even the immovable man of science had a bright, bewildered sensation that the Time Machine had given a great jerk, and gone forward with rather rattling rapidity.

He was not, however, wholly prepared for what happened next. The man in green, riding the frail topmost bough like a witch on a very risky broomstick, reached up and rent the black hat from its airy nest of twigs. It had been broken across a heavy bough in the first burst of its passage, a tangle of branches had torn and scored and scratched it in every direction, a clap of wind and foliage had flattened it like a concertina; nor can it be said that the obliging gentleman with the sharp nose showed any adequate tenderness for its structure when he finally unhooked it from its place. When he had found it, however, his proceedings were by some counted singular. He waved it with a loud whoop of triumph, and then immediately appeared to fall backwards off the tree, to which, however, he remained attached by his long strong legs, like a monkey swung by his tail. Hanging thus head downwards above the unhelmed Warner, he gravely proceeded to drop the battered silk cylinder upon his brows. "Every man a king," explained the inverted philosopher; "every hat (consequently) a crown. But this is a crown out of heaven."

And he again attempted the coronation of Warner, who, however, moved away with great abruptness from the hovering diadem; not seeming, strangely enough, to wish for his former decoration in its present state.

"Wrong, wrong!" cried the obliging person hilariously. "Always wear uniform, even if it's shabby uniform! Ritualists may always be untidy. Go to a dance with soot on your shirt-front; but go with a shirt-front. Huntsman wears old coat; but old pink coat. Wear a topper, even if it's got no top. It's the symbol that counts, old cock. Take your hat, because it is your hat after all; its nap rubbed all off by the bark, dears, and its brim not the least bit curled; but for old sakes' sake it is still, dears, the nobbiest tile in the world."

Speaking thus, with a wild comfortableness, he settled or smashed the shapeless silk hat over the face of the disturbed physician, and fell on his feet among the other men, still talking, beaming and breathless.

"Why don't they make more games out of the wind?" he asked in some excitement. "Kites are all right, but why should it only be kites? Why, I thought of three other games for a windy day while I was climbing that tree. Here's one of them: you take a lot of pepper—"

"I think," interposed Moon, with a sardonic mildness, "that your games are already sufficiently interesting. Are you, may I ask, a professional acrobat on a tour, or a travelling advertisement of Sunny Jim? How and why do you display all this energy for clearing walls and climbing trees in our melancholy, but at least rational, suburbs ?"

The stranger, so far as so loud a person was capable of it, appeared to grow confidential.

"Well, it's a trick of my own," he confessed candidly. "I do it by having two legs."

Arthur Inglewood who had sunk into the background of this scene of folly, started and stared at the newcomer with his shortsighted eyes screwed up and his high colour fiercely heightened.

"Why, I believe you're Smith," he cried with his fresh, almost boyish voice; and then after an instant's stare, "and yet I'm not sure."

"I have a card, I think," said the unknown, with baffling solemnity; "a card with my real name, my titles, offices, and true purpose on this earth."

He drew out slowly from an upper waistcoat pocket a scarlet card-case, and as slowly produced a very large card. Even in the instant of its production, they fancied it was of a queer shape, unlike the cards of ordinary gentlemen. But it was there only for an instant; for as it passed from his fingers to Arthur's, one or other slipped his hold. The strident, tearing gale in that garden carried away the stranger's card to join the wild waste-paper of the universe; and that great, western wind shook the whole house and passed.

## CHAPTER II

## THE LUGGAGE OF AN OPTIMIST

WE all remember the fairy tales of science in our infancy, which played with the supposition that large animals could jump in the proportion of small ones. If an elephant were as strong as a grasshopper, he could (I suppose) spring clean out of the Zoological Gardens and alight trumpeting upon Primrose Hill. If a whale could leap from the water like a trout, perhaps men might look up and see one soaring above Yarmouth like the winged island of Laputa. Such natural energy, though sublime, might certainly be inconvenient, and much of this inconvenience attended the gaiety and good intentions of the man in green. He was too large for everything, because he was lively as well as large. By a fortunate physical provision most very substantial creatures are also reposeful; and middle class boarding-houses in the lesser parti of London are not built for a man as big at a bull, and as excitable as a kitten.

When Inglewood followed the stranger into the boarding-house, he found him talking earnestly and (in his own opinion) privately to the helpless Mrs. Duke. That fat, faint lady could only goggle up like a dying fish at the enormous new gentleman, who politely offered himself as lodger, with vast gestures of the wide white hat in one hand, and the yellow Gladstone bag in the other. Fortunately, Mrs. Duke's more efficient niece and partner was there to complete the contract; for, indeed, all the people of the house had somehow collected in the room. This fact in truth was typical of the whole episode. The visitor created an atmosphere of comic crisis; and from the time he came into the house to the time he left it, he somehow got the company to gather and even follow (though in derision), as children gather and follow a Punch and Judy. An hour ago, and for four years previously, these people had avoided each other, even when they really liked each other. They had slid in and out of dismal and deserted rooms in search of particular newspapers or private needlework. Even now they all came casually, as with varying interests; but they all came. There was the embarrassed Inglewood, still a sort of red shadow; there also the unembarrassed Warner, a pallid, but solid substance. There was Michael Moon offering like a riddle the contrast of the horsy crudeness of his clothes, and the sombre sagacity of his visage. He was now joined by his yet more comic crony, Moses Gould. Swaggering on short legs with a prosperous purple tie, he was the gayest of godless little dogs; but like a dog also in this, that however he danced and wagged with delight, the two dark eyes on each side of his protuberant nose glistened gloomily like black buttons. There was Miss Rosamund Hunt, still with the fine white hat framing her square, good-humoured face; and still with her native air of being dressed for some party that never came off. She also, like Mr. Moon, had a new companion, new so far as this narrative goes, but in reality an old friend and protegee. This was a slight, young woman in black, and in no way notable but for a load of dull red hair, of which the shape somehow gave her pale face that triangular, almost peaked appearance which was given by the lowering headdress and deep rich ruff of the Elizabethan beauties. Her surname seemed to be Gray, and Miss Hunt called her Mary, in that indescribable tone applied to an old dependent who has practically become a friend. She wore a small silver cross on her very businesslike black clothes, and was the only member of the party who went to church. Last, but the reverse of least, there was Diana Duke, studying the newcomer with eyes of steel, and listening carefully to every idiotic word he said. As for Mrs. Duke, she smiled up at him; but never dreamed of listening to him. She had never really listened to any one in her life; which some said was why she had survived.

Nevertheless, Mrs. Duke was pleased with her new guest's concentration of courtesy upon herself; for no one ever spoke seriously to her any more than she listened seriously to any one. And she almost beamed as the stranger, with yet wider and almost whirling gestures of explanation with his huge hat and bag, apologized for having entered by the wall instead of the front door. He was understood to put it down to an unfortunate family tradition of neatness and care of his clothes.

"My mother was rather strict about it, to tell the truth," he said, lowering his voice, to Mrs. Duke. "She never liked me to lose my cap at school. And when a man's been taught to be tidy and neat it sticks to him."

Mrs. Duke weakly gasped that she was sure he must have had a good mother; but her niece seemed inclined to probe the matter further.

"You've got a funny idea of tidiness," she said, "if it's jumping garden walls and clambering up garden trees. A man can't very well climb a tree tidily."

"He can clear a wall neatly," said Michael Moon; "I saw him do it."

Smith seemed to be regarding the girl with genuine astonishment. "My dear young lady," he said, "I was tidying the tree. You don't want last year's hats there, do you, any more than last year's leaves. The wind takes off the leaves, but it couldn't manage the hat; that wind, I suppose, has tidied whole forests to-day. Rum idea this is, that tidiness is a timid, quiet sort of thing; why, tidiness is a toil for giants. You can't tidy anything without untidying yourself; just look at my trousers. Don't you know that? Haven't you ever had a spring cleaning?"

"Oh, yes, sir," said Mrs. Duke, almost eagerly. "You will find everything of that sort quite nice." For the first time she had heard two words that she could understand.

Miss Diana Duke seemed to be studying the stranger in a sort of spasm of calculation; then her black eyes snapped with decision, and she said that he could have a particular bedroom on the top floor if he liked, and the silent and sensitive Inglewood, who had been on the rack through these cross purposes, eagerly offered to show him up to the room. Smith went up the stairs four at a time, and when he bumped his head against the ultimate ceiling, Inglewood had an odd sensation that the tall house was much shorter than it used to be.

Arthur Inglewood followed his old friend —or his new friend—for he did not very clearly know which he was. The face looked very like his old schoolfellow's at one second and very unlike at another.

And when Inglewood broke through his native politeness so far as to say suddenly, "Is your name Smith?" he received only the un-enlightening reply, "Quite right. Quite right. Very good. Excellent I" Which appeared to Inglewood, on reflection, rather the speech of a new-born babe accepting a name, than of a grown-up man admitting one.

Despite this double about identity, the hapless Inglewood watched the other unpack, and stood about his bedroom in all the important attitudes of the male friend. Mr. Smith unpacked with the same kind of whirling accuracy with which he climbed a tree; throwing things out of his bag as if they were rubbish, yet managing to distribute quite a regular pattern all round him on the floor.

As he did so he continued to talk in the same somewhat gasping manner (he had come upstairs four steps at a time, but even without this his style of speech was breathless and fragmentary) ; and his remarks were still a string of more or less significant but often separate pictures.

"Like the day of judgment," he said, throwing a bottle so that it somehow settled, rocking on its right end. "People say vast universe . . . infinity and astronomy; not sure ... I think things are too close together . . . packed up; for travelling . . . stars too close really . . . why, the sun's a star, too close to be seen properly; the earth's a star, too close to be seen at all . . . too many pebbles on the beach; ought all to be put in rings; too many blades of grass to study . . . feathers on a bird make the brain reel; wait till the big bag is unpacked . . . may all be put in our right places then."

Here he stopped, literally for breath; throwing a shirt to the other end of the room, and then a bottle of ink so that it fell quite neatly beyond it. Inglewood looked round on this strange, half-symmetrical disorder with an increasing doubt.

In fact, the more one explored Mr. Smith's holiday luggage, the less one could make anything of it. One peculiarity of it was that almost everything seemed to be there for the wrong reason; what is secondary with every one else was primary with him. He would wrap up a pot or pan in brown paper; and the 3 33 unthinking assistant would discover that the pot was valueless or even unnecessary, and that it was the brown paper that was truly precious. He produced two or three boxes of cigars, and explained with plain perplexing sincerity that he was no smoker, but that cigar-box wood was by far the best for fretwork. He also exhibited about six small bottles of wine, white and red; and Inglewood, happening to note a Volnay which he knew to be excellent, supposed at first that the stranger was an epicure in vintages. He was therefore surprised to find that the next bottle was a vile sham claret from the colonies, which even colonials (to do them justice) do not drink.

It was only then that he observed that all six bottles had those bright metallic seals of various tints, and seemed to have been chosen solely because they gave the three primary and three secondary colours: red, blue, and yellow; green, violet, and orange. There grew upon Inglewood an almost creepy sense of the real childishness of this creature. For Smith was really, so far as human psychology can be, innocent. He had the sensualities of innocence; he loved the stickiness of

gum and he cut white wood greedily as if he were cutting a cake. To this man wine was not a doubtful thing to be defended or denounced; it was a quaintly-coloured syrup, such as a child sees in a shop window. He talked dominantly and rushed the social situation; but he was not asserting himself, like a superman in a modern play. He was simply forgetting himself, like a little boy at a party. He had somehow made a giant stride from babyhood to manhood, and missed that crisis in youth when most of us grow old.

As he shunted his big bag, Arthur observed the initials I. S. printed on one side of it, and remembered that Smith had been called Innocent Smith at school, though whether as a formal Christian name or a moral description he could not remember. He was just about to venture another question, when there was a knock at the door, and the short figure of Mr. Gould offered itself, with the melancholy Moon, standing like his tall crooked shadow, behind him. They had drifted up the stairs after the other two men with the wandering gregariousness of the male.

"Hope there's no intrusion," said the beam-

ing Moses with a glow of good nature, but not the airiest tinge of apology.

"The truth is," said Michael Moon with comparative courtesy, "we thought we might see if they had made you comfortable. Miss Duke is rather—"

"I know," cried the stranger, looking up radiantly from his bag; "magnificent isn't she? Go close to her—hear military music going by, like Joan of Arc."

Inglewood started and stared at the speaker like one who has just heard a wild fairy tale, which nevertheless contains one small and forgotten fact. For he remembered how he had himself thought of Jeanne d'Arc years ago, when, hardly more than a schoolboy, he had first come to the boarding-house. Long since the pulverizing rationalism of his friend Dr. Warner had crushed such youthful ignorances and disproportionate dreams. Under the Warnerian scepticism and science of hopeless human types, Inglewood had long come to regard himself as a timid, insufficient, and "weak" type, who would never marry; to regard Diana Duke as a materialistic maidservant; and to regard his first fancy for her as the

small, dull farce of a collegian kissing his landlady's daughter. And yet the phrase about military music moved him queerly; as if he had heard those distant drums.

"She has to keep things pretty tight, as is only natural," said Moon, glancing round the rather dwarfish room, with its wedge of slanted ceiling, like the conical hood of a dwarf.

"Rather a small box for you, sir," said the waggish Mr. Gould.

"Splendid room, though," answered Mr. Smith enthusiastically, with his head beside his Gladstone bag. "I love these pointed sorts of rooms, like Gothic. By the way," he cried out, pointing in quite a startling way. "Where does that door lead to?"

"To certain death, I should say," answered Michael Moon, staring up at a dust-stained and disused trap-door in the sloping roof of the attic. "I don't think there's a loft there; and I don't know what else it could lead to." Long before he had finished his sentence, the man with the strong green legs had leapt at the door in the ceiling, swung himself somehow on to the ledge beneath it, wrenched it open after a 8truggle, and clambered through it For a moment they saw the two symbolic legs standing like a truncated statue, then they vanished. Through the hole thus burst in the roof appeared the empty and lucid sky of evening, with one great many-coloured cloud sailing across it like a whole county upside down.

"Hullo, you fellows!" came the far cry of Innocent Smith, apparently from some remote pinnacle. "Come up here; and bring some of my things to eat and drink. It's just the spot for a picnic."

With a sudden impulse Michael snatched two of the small wine bottles, one in each solid fist; and Arthur Inglewood, as if mesmerized, groped for a biscuit tin and a big jar of ginger. The enormous hand of Innocent Smith appearing through the aperture, like a giant's in a fairy tale, received these tributes and bore them off to the eyrie, then they both hoisted themselves out of the window. They were both athletic, and even gymnastic; Inglewood through his concern for hygiene, and Moon through his concern for sport, which was not quite so idle and inactive as that of the average iportsman. Also they both had a light-headed, celestial sensation when the door was burst in the roof, as if a door had been burst in the sky, and they could climb on to the very roof of the universe. They were both men who had long been consciously imprisoned in the commonplace, though one took it comically, and the other seriously. They were both men, nevertheless, in whom sentiment had never died. But Mr. Moses Gould had an equal contempt for their suicidal athletics and their subconscious transcendentalism, and he stood and laughed at the thing with the shameless rationality of another race.

When the singular Smith, astride of a chimney-pot, learnt that Gould was not following, his infantile officiousness and good-nature forced him to dive back into the attic to comfort or persuade; and Inglewood and Moon were left alone on the long gray-green ridge of the slate roof, with their feet against gutters and their backs against chimney-pots, looking agnostically at each other. Their first feeling was that they had come out into eternity; and that eternity was very like topsy-turvydom. One definition occurred to one of them; that he had come out into the light of that lucid and radiant ignorance in which all beliefs had begun. The sky above them was full of mythology. Heaven seemed deep enough to hold all the gods. The round of the ether turned from green to yellow gradually like a great unripe fruit. All around the sunken sun it was like a lemon; round all the east it was a sort of golden green, more suggestive of a greengage; but the whole had still the emptiness of daylight and none of the secrecy of dusk. Tumbled here and there across this gold and pale green were shards and shattered masses of inky purple cloud, which seemed falling towards the earth in every kind of colossal perspective. One of them really had the character of some many-mitred, many-bearded, many-winged Assyrian image, huge head downwards, hurled out of heaven; a sort of false Jehovah, who was perhaps Satan. All the other clouds had preposterous pinnacled shapes; as if the god's palaces had been flung after him.

And yet, while the empty heaven was full of silent catastrophe, the height of human buildings above which they sat held here and there a tiny and trivial noise that was the exact antithesis; and they heard some six streets below a newsboy calling, and a bell bidding to chapel. They could also hear talk out of the garden below; and realized that the irrepressible Smith must have followed Gould downstairs, for his eager and pleading accents could be heard, followed by the half-humorous protests of Miss Duke, and the full and very youthful laughter of Rosamund Hunt. The air had that cold kindness that comes after a storm. Michael Moon drank it in with as serious a relish as he had drunk the little bottle of cheap claret, which he had emptied almost at a draught. Inglewood went on eating ginger very slowly and with a solemnity unfathomable as the sky above him. There was still enough stir in the freshness of the atmosphere to make them almost fancy they could smell the garden soil and the last roses of the autumn. Suddenly there came from the darkening garden a silvery ping and pong which told them that Rosamund had brought out the long-neglected mandoline. After the first few notes there was more of the distant bell-like laughter.

MAN ALIVE

"Inglewood," said Michael Moon, "have you ever heard that I am a blackguard?"

"I haven't heard it, and I don't believe it," answered Inglewood, after an odd pause. "But I have heard you were—what they call rather wild."

"If you have heard that I am wild, you can contradict the rumour," said Moon, with an extraordinary calm; "I am tame. I am quite tame; I am about the tamest beast that crawls. I drink too much of the same kind of whiskey at the same time every night. I even drink about the same amount too much. I go to the same number of public-houses. I meet the same damned women with mauve faces. I /hear the same number of dirty stories—generally the same dirty stories. You may reassure my friends, Inglewood, you see before you a person whom civilization has thoroughly tamed."

Arthur Inglewood was staring with feelings that made him nearly fall off the roof; for indeed the Irishman's face, always sinister, was now almost demoniacal.

"Christ confound it," cried out Moon, suddenly clutching the empty claret bottle, "this

MANALIVE

is about the thinnest and filthiest wine I ever uncorked, and it's the only drink I have really enjoyed for nine years. I was never wild until just ten minutes ago." And he sent the bottle whizzing, a wheel of glass, far away beyond the garden into the road, where, in the enormous evening silence, they could even hear it break and part upon the stones.

"Moon," said Arthur Inglewood, rather huskily, "you mustn't be so bitter about it—everybody has to take the world as he finds it, of course one often finds it a bit dull—"

"That fellow doesn't," said Michael decisively; "I mean that fellow Smith. I have a fancy there's some method in his madness. It looks as if he could turn into a sort of wonderland any minute by taking one step out of the plain road. Who would have thought of that trap-door? Who would have thought that this cursed colonial claret could taste quite nice among the chimney-pots? Perhaps that is the real key of fairyland. Perhaps Nosey Gould's beastly little Empire cigarettes ought only to be smoked on stilts, or somewhere of that sort. Perhaps Mrs. Duke's cold leg of mutton would seem quite appetizing at the top

MANALIVE

of a tree. Perhaps even my damned, dirty, monotonous drizzle of old Bill Whiskey—"

"Don't be rough on yourself," said Ingle-wood, in serious distress. "The dullness isn't your fault or the whiskey's. Fellows who don't—fellows like me I mean—have just the same feeling that it's all rather flat at a failure. But the world's made like that; it's all survival. Some people are made to get on, like Warner, and some people are made to stick quiet, like me. You can't help your temperament. I know you're much cleverer than I am; but you can't help having all the loose ways of a poor literary chap, and I can't help having all the doubts and helplessness of a small scientific chap, any more than a fish can help floating, or a fern help curling up. Humanity, as Warner said so well in that lecture, really consists of quite different tribes of animals all disguised as men."

In the dim garden below, the buzz of talk was suddenly broken by Miss Hunt's musical instrument banging with the abruptness of artillery into a vulgar but spirited tune.

Rosamund's voice came up rich and strong 44

MANALIVE

in the words of some fatuous, fashionable coon song—

"Darkies sing a song on the old plantation, Sing it as we sang it in the days long since gone by."

InglewoocTs brown eyes softened and saddened still more as he continued his monologue of resignation to such a rollicking and romantic tune. But the blue eyes of Michael Moon brightened and hardened with a light that Inglewood did not understand. Many centuries, and many villages and valleys, would have been happier if Inglewood or Ingle-wood's countrymen had ever understood that light, or guessed at the first blink that it was the battle star of Ireland.

"Nothing can ever alter it, it's in the wheels of the universe," went on Inglewood, in a low voice; "some men are weak and some strong, and the only thing we can do is to know that we are weak. I have been in love lots of times, but I could not do anything for I remembered my own fickleness. I have formed opinions, but I haven't the cheek to push them, because I've so often changed

MANALIVE

them. That's the upshot, old fellow. We can't trust ourselves, and we can't help it."

Michael had risen to his feet, and stood poised in the perilous position at the end of the roof, like some dark statue hung above its gable. Behind him, huge clouds of an almost impossible purple turned slowly topsy-turvy in the silent anarchy of heaven. Their gyration made the dark figure seem yet dizzier.

"Let us . . ." he said, and was suddenly silent.

"Let us what?" asked Arthur Inglewood, rising equally quickly though somewhat more cautiously, for his friend seemed to find some difficulty of speech.

"Let us go and do some of these things we can't do," said Michael.

At that same moment there burst out of the trap-door below them, the cockatoo hair and flushed face of Innocent Smith, calling to them that they must come down as the "concert" was in full swing, and Mr. Moses Gould about to recite "Young Lochinvar."

As they dropped into Innocent's attic they nearly tumbled over its entertaining impedimenta again. Inglewood, staring at the lit-

MANALIVE

tered floor, thought instinctively of the littered floor of a nursery. He was, therefore, the more moved, and even shocked, when his eye fell on a large well-polished American revolver.

"Hullo," he cried, stepping back from the steely glitter, as men step back from a serpent; "are you afraid of burglars, or when and why do you deal death out of that machine gun?"

"Oh, that!" said Smith, throwing it a single glance; "I deal life out of that," and he went bounding down the stairs.

CHAPTER III

## THE BANNER OF BEACON

ALL next day at Beacon House there was •*-*- a crazy sense that it was everybody's birthday. It is the fashion to talk of institutions as cold and cramping things. The truth is that when people are in exceptionally high spirits, really wild with freedom and invention, they always must, and they always do, create institutions. When men are weary they fall into anarchy; but while they are gay and vigorous they invariably make rules. This, which is true of all the churches and republics of history, is also true of the most trivial parlour game or the most unsophisticated meadow romp. We are never free until some institution frees us; and liberty cannot exist till it is declared by authority. Even the wild authority of the harlequin Smith was still authority, because it produced everywhere a crop of crazy regulations and conditions.

MANALIVE

He filled every one with his own half-lunatic life; but it was not expressed in destruction, but rather in a dizzy and toppling construction. Each person with a hobby found it turning into an institution. Rosamund's songs seemed to coalesce into a kind of opera; Michael's jests and paragraphs into a magazine. His pipe and her mandoline seemed between them to make a sort of smoking concert. The bashful and bewildered Arthur Ingle-wood almost struggled against his own growing importance. He felt as if, in spite of him, his photographs were turning into a picture gallery, and his bicycle into a gymkana. But no one had any time to criticize these impromptu estates and offices, for they followed each other in wild succession like the topics of a rambling talker.

Existence with such a man was an obstacle race made of pleasant obstacles. Out of any homely and trivial object he could drag reels of exaggeration, like a conjuror. Nothing could be more shy and impersonal than poor Arthur's photography. Yet the preposterous « Smith was seen assisting him eagerly through sunny morning hours, and an indefensible

MANALIVE

sequence described as "Moral Photography" began to unroll itself about the boarding-house. It was only a version of the old photographer's joke which produces the same figure twice on one plate, making a man play chess with himself, dine with himself, and so on. But these plates were more mystical and ambitious; as "Miss Hunt forgets Herself," showing that lady answering her own too rapturous recognition with a most appalling stare of ignorance; or "Mr. Moon questions Himself," in which Mr. Moon appeared as one driven to madness under his own legal cross-examination, which was conducted with a long forefinger and an air of ferocious waggery. One highly successful trilogy—representing Inglewood recognizing Inglewood, Inglewood prostrating himself before Inglewood, and Inglewood severely beating Inglewood with an umbrella —Innocent Smith wanted to have enlarged and put up in the hall, like a sort of fresco, with the inscription—

"Self-knowledge, self-reverence, self-control: These three alone will make a man a prig."
Tennyson.

MANALIVE

Nothing, again, could be more prosaic and impenetrable than the domestic energies of Miss Diana Duke. But Innocent had somehow blundered on the discovery that her thrifty dressmaking went with a considerable feminine care for dress—the one feminine thing that had never failed her solitary self-respect. In consequence Smith pestered her with a theory (which he really seemed to take seriously) that ladies might combine economy with magnificence if they would draw light chalk patterns on a plain dress and then dust them off again. He set up "Smith's Lightning Dressmaking Company" with two screens, a cardboard placard, and box of bright soft crayons; and Miss Diana actually threw him an abandoned black overall or working dress on which to exercise the talents of a modiste. He promptly produced for her a garment aflame with red and gold sunflowers; she held it up an instant to her shoulders, and looked like an empress. And Arthur Inglewood, some hours afterwards cleaning his bicycle (with his usual air of being inextricably hidden in it), glanced up, and his hot face grew hotter, for Diana stood laughing for one flash in the doorway, and her dark robe was rich with the green and purple of great decorative peacocks, like a secret garden in the Arabian Nights. A pang, too swift to be named pain or pleasure, went through his heart like an old-world rapier. He remembered how pretty he thought her years ago, when he was ready to fall in love with anybody; but it was like remembering a worship of some Babylonian princess in some previous existence. At his next glimpse of her (and he caught himself awaiting it), the purple and green chalk was dusted off, and she went by quickly in her working clothes.

As for Mrs. Duke, none who knew that matron could conceive her as actively resisting this invasion that had turned her house upside down. But among the most exact observers it was seriously believed that she liked it. For she was one of those women who at bottom regard all men as equally mad, wild animals of some utterly separate species. And it is doubtful if she really saw anything more eccentric or inexplicable in Smith's chimney-pot picnics or crimson sunflowers than she had in the chemicals of Inglewood or the sardonic speeches of Moon. Courtesy, on the other hand, is a thing that any one can understand; and Smith's manners were as courteous as they were unconventional. She said he was "a real gentleman," by which she simply meant a kind-hearted man, which is a very different thing. She would sit at the head of the table with fat, folded hands and a fat, folded smile for hours and hours, while every one else was talking at once. At least, the only other exception was Rosamund's companion, Mary Gray, whose silence was of a much more eager sort. Though she never spoke she always looked as if she might speak any minute. Perhaps this is the very definition of a companion. Innocent Smith seemed to throw himself, as into other adventures, into the adventure of making her talk. He never succeeded, yet he was never snubbed; if he achieved anything, it was only to draw attention to this quiet figure, and to turn her, by ever so little, from a modesty to a mystery. But if she was a riddle, every one recognized that she was a fresh and unspoilt riddle, like the riddle of the sky and the woods in spring. Indeed, though she was rather older than the other two girls, she had an early morning ardour, a fresh earnestness of youth, which Rosamund seemed to have lost in the mere spending of money, and Diana in the mere guarding of it. Smith looked at her again and again. Her eyes and mouth were set in her face the wrong way which was really the right way. She had the knack of saying everything with her face; her silence was a sort of steady applause.

But among the hilarious experiments of that holiday (which seemed more like a week's holiday than a day's) one experiment towers supreme, not because it was any sillier or more successful than the others, but because out of this particular folly flowed all the odd events that were to follow. All the other practical jokes exploded of themselves and left vacancy; all the other fictions returned upon themselves and were finished, like a song. But the string of solid and startling events—which were to include a hansom cab, a detective, a pistol, and a marriage licence—were all made primarily possible by the joke about the High Court of Beacon.

It had originated not with Innocent Smith, but with Michael Moon. He was in a strange glow and pressure of spirits, and talked incessantly; yet he had never been more sarcastic, and even inhuman. He used his old useless knowledge as a barrister to talk entertainingly of a tribunal that was a parody on the pompous anomalies of English law. The High Court of Beacon, he declared, was a splendid example of our free and sensible constitution. It had been founded by King John in defiance of Magna Charta, and now held absolute power over windmills, wine and spirit licences, ladies travelling in Turkey, revision of sentences for dog-stealing and parricide, as well as anything whatever that happened in the town of Market-Bosworth. The whole hundred and nine seneschals of the High Court of Beacon met once in every four centuries; but in the intervals (as Mr. Moon explained) the whole powers of the institution were vested in Mrs. Duke. Tossed about among the rest of the company, however, the

High Court did not retain its historical and legal seriousness, but was used somewhat unscrupulously in a riot of domestic detail. If somebody spilt the Worcester sauce on the tablecloth, he was quite sure it was a rite without which the sittings and findings of the Court would be invalid; or if somebody wanted a window to remain shut, he would suddenly remember that none but the third son of the lord of the manor of Penge had the right to open it. They even went the length of making arrests and conducting criminal inquiries. The proposed trial of Moses Gould for patriotism was rather above the heads of the company, especially of the criminal; but the trial of Inglewood on a charge of photographic libel, and his triumphant acquittal upon a plea of insanity, were admitted to be in the best traditions of the Court.

But when Smith was in wild spirits he grew more and more serious, not more and more flippant like Michael Moon. This proposal of a private court of justice which Moon had thrown off with the detachment of a political humorist, Smith really caught

hold of with the eagerness of an abstract philosopher. It was by far the best thing they could do, he declared, to claim sovereign powers even for the individual household.

"You believe in Home Rule for Ireland; I believe in Home Rule for homes," he cried eagerly to Michael. "It would be better if every father could kill his son, as with the old Romans—it would be better, because nobody would be killed. Let's issue a Declaration of Independence from Beacon House. We could grow enough greens in that garden to support us, and when the tax-collector comes let's tell him we're self-supporting, and play on him with the hose. . . . Well, perhaps, as you say, we couldn't very well have a hose, as that comes from the main; but we could sink a well in this chalk, and a lot could be done with water-jugs. . . . Let this be really Beacon House. Let's light a bonfire of independence on the roof, and see house after house answering it across the valley of the Thames! Let us begin the League of the Free Families! Away with Local Government! A fig for

Local Patriotism! Let every house be a sovereign state as this is, and judge its own children by its own law, as we do by the Court of Beacon! Let us cut the painter, and begin to be happy together, as if we were on a desert island!"

"I know that desert island," said Michael Moon; "it only exists in the 'Swiss Family Robinson.' A man feels a strange desire for some sort of vegetable milk, and crash comes down some unexpected cocoanut from some undiscovered monkey. A literary man feels inclined to pen a sonnet, and at once an officious porcupine rushes out of a thicket, and shoots out one of his quills."

"Don't you say a word against the 'Swiss Family Robinson,' " cried Innocent with great warmth. "It mayn't be exact science, but it's dead accurate philosophy. When you're really shipwrecked, you do really find what you want. When you're really on a desert island, you never find it a desert. If we were really besieged in this garden we'd find a hundred English birds and English berries that we never knew were here. If we were snowed up in this room, we'd be the better for reading scores of books in that bookcase that we don't even know are there; we'd have talks with each other; good, terrible talks, that we shall go to the grave without guessing; we'd find materials for everything: christening, marriage or funeral—yes, even for a Coronation, if we didn't decide to be a republic."

"A Coronation on 'Swiss Family' lines, I suppose," said Michael, laughing. "Oh, I know you would find everything in that atmosphere. If we wanted such a simple thing, for instance, as a Coronation Canopy, we should walk down beyond the geraniums and find the Canopy Tree in full bloom. If we wanted such a trifle as a crown of gold, why, we should be digging up dandelions, and we should find a gold mine under the lawn. And when we wanted oil for the ceremony, why, I suppose, a great storm would wash everything on shore, and we should find there was a whale on the premises."

"And so there is a whale on the premises for all you know," asseverated Smith, striking the table with passion. "I bet you've never examined the premises! I bet you've never been round at the back as I was this morning—for I found the very thing you say could only grow on a tree. There's an old sort of square tent up against the dustbin; it's got three holes in the canvas, and a pole's broken, so it's not much good as a tent, but as a Canopy—" And his voice quite failed him to express its shining adequacy; then he went on with controversial eagerness. "You see I take every challenge as you make it. I believe every blessed thing you say couldn't be here has been here all the time. You say you want a whale washed up for oil. Why, there's oil in that cruet-stand at your elbow; and I don't believe anybody has touched it or thought of it for years. And for your gold crown, we're none of us wealthy here, but we could collect enough ten shilling bits from our own pockets to string round a man's head for half an hour; or one of Miss Hunt's gold bangles is nearly big enough to—"

The good-humoured Rosamund was almost choking with laughter. "All is not gold that glitters," she said; "and besides—"

"What a mistake that is!" cried Innocent Smith, leaping up in great excitement. "All is gold that glitters—especially now we are a Sovereign State. What's the good of a Sovereign State if it can't define a sovereign? We can make anything a precious metal, as men could in the morning of the world. They didn't choose gold because it was rare—your scientists can tell you twenty sorts of slime much rarer. They chose gold because it was bright—because it was a thing hard to find— but pretty when you've found it. You can't fight with golden swords or eat golden biscuits; you can only look at it—and you can look at it out here."

With one of his incalculable motions he sprang back and burst open the doors into the garden. At the same time, also, with one of his gestures that never seemed at the instant so unconventional as they were, he stretched out his hand to Mary Gray, and led her out on to the lawn as if for a dance.

The French windows, thus flung open, let in an evening even lovelier than that of the day before. The west was swimming with sanguine colours, and a sort of sleepy flame lay along the lawn. The twisted shadows of the one or two garden trees showed upon this sheen, not gray or black, as in common day- light, but like arabesques written in vivid violet ink on some page of eastern gold. The sunset was one of those festive, and yet mysterious conflagrations in which common things by their colours remind us of costly or curious things. The slates upon the sloping roof burned like the plumes of a vast peacock, in every mysterious blend of blue and green. The red-brown bricks of the wall glowed with all the October tints of strong ruby and tawny wines. The sun seemed to set each object alight with a different coloured flame, like a man lighting fireworks; and even Innocent's hair, which was of a rather colourless fairness, seemed to have a flame of pagan gold on it as he strode across the lawn towards the one tall ridge of rockery.

"What would be the good of gold," he was saying, "if it did not glitter? Why should we care for a black sovereign any more than a black sun at noon? A black button would do just as well. Don't you see that everything in this yard looks like a jewel? And will you kindly tell me what the deuce is the good of a jewel except that it looks like a jewel? Leave off buying and selling, and start looking! Open your eyes; and you'll wake up in the New Jerusalem."

"All is gold that glitters:
Tree and tower of brass Rolls the golden evening air
Down the golden grass; Kick the cry to Jericho,
How yellow mud is sold; All is gold that glitters,
For the glitter is the gold."

"And who wrote that?" asked Rosamund, amused.

"No one will ever write it," answered Smith, and cleared the rockery with a flying leap.

"Really," said Rosamund to Michael Moon, "he ought to be sent to an asylum. Don't you think so?"

"I beg your pardon," inquired Michael, rather sombrely; his long, swarthy head was dark against the sunset, and either by accident or mood he had the look of something isolated and even hostile amid the social extravagance of the garden.

"I only said Mr. Smith ought to go to an asylum," repeated the lady.

*3

The lean face seemed to grow longer and longer; for Moon was unmistakably sneering. "No," he said; "I don't think it's at all necessary."

"What do you mean?" asked Rosamund quickly. "Why not?"

"Because he is in one now," answered Michael Moon in a quiet but ugly voice. "Why, didn't you know?"

"What?" cried the girl, and there was a break in her voice; for the Irishman's face and voice were really almost creepy. With his dark figure and dark sayings in all that sunshine he looked like the devil in paradise.

"I'm sorry," he continued, with a sort of harsh humility. "Of course we don't talk about it much . . . but I thought we all really knew."

"Knew what?"

"Well," answered Moon, "that Beacon House is a certain rather singular sort of house. A house with the tiles loose, shall we say? Innocent Smith is only the doctor that visits us; hadn't you come when he called before? As most of our maladies are melancholic, of course he has to be extra cheery. Sanity, of course, seems a very bumptious eccentric thing to us. Jumping over a wall — climbing a tree—that's his bedside manner."

"You daren't say such a thing!" cried Rosamund in a rage. "You daren't suggest that I—"

"Not more than I am," said Michael soothingly. "Not more than the rest of us. Haven't you ever noticed that Miss Duke never sits still—a notorious sign? Haven't you ever observed that Inglewood is always washing his hands—a known mark of mental disease. I, of course, am a dipsomaniac."

"I don't believe you," broke out his companion, not without agitation. "I've heard you had some bad habits—"

"All habits are bad habits," said Michael, with deadly calm. "Madness does not come by breaking out, but by giving in; by settling down in some dirty, little, self-repeating circle of ideas; by being tamed. You went mad about money, because you're an heiress."

"It's a lie," cried Rosamund furiously. "I never was mean about money."

"You were worse," said Michael, in a low voice, and yet violently. "You thought that other people were. You thought every man who came near you must be a fortune-hunter; .you would not let yourself go and be sane; and now you're mad, and I'm mad; and serve us right."

"You brute," said Rosamund quite white. "And is this true?"

With an intellectual cruelty of which the Celt is capable when his abysses are in revolt, Michael was silent for some seconds, and then stepped back with an ironical bow. "Not literally true, of course," he said; "only really true. An allegory, shall we say? A social satire."

"And I hate and despise your satires," cried Rosamund Hunt, letting loose her whole forcible female personality like a cyclone; and speaking every word to wound. "I despise it as I despise your rank tobacco, and your nasty, loungy ways, and your snarling, and your Radicalism, and your old clothes, and your potty little newspaper, and your rotten failure at everything. I don't care whether you call it snobbishness or not, I like life and success, and jolly things to look at, and action. You won't frighten me with Diogenes; I prefer Alexander."

"Victrix causa dex —" said Michael gloomily, and this angered her more, as, not knowing what it meant, she imagined it to be witty.

"Oh, I dare say you know Greek," she said, with cheerful inaccuracy; "you haven't done much with that either," and she crossed the garden, pursuing the vanished Innocent and Mary.

In doing so she passed Inglewood, who was returning to the house slowly, and with a thought-clouded brow. He was one of those men who are quite clever, but quite the reverse of quick. As he came back out of the sunset garden into the twilight parlour, Diana Duke slipt swiftly to her feet, and began putting away the tea things. But it was not before Inglewood had seen an instantaneous picture so unique, that he might well have snapshotted it with his everlasting camera. For Diana had been sitting in front of her unfinished work with her chin on her hand, looking straight out of the window in pure thoughtless thought.

"You are busy," said Arthur, oddly embarrassed with what he had seen, and wishing to ignore it.

"There's no time for dreaming in this world," answered the young lady with her back to him.

"I have been thinking lately," said Inglewood in a low voice, "that there's no time for waking up."

She did not reply, and he walked to the window and looked out on the garden.

"I don't smoke or drink you know," he said irrelevantly, "because I think they're drugs. And yet I fancy all hobbies, like my camera and bicycle, are drugs too. Getting under a black hood, getting into a dark room—getting into a hole anyhow. Drugging myself with speed, and sunshine, and fatigue, and fresh air. Pedalling the machine so fast that I turn into a machine myself. That's the matter with all of us. We're too busy to wake up."

"Well," said the girl solidly, "what is there to wake up to?"

"There must be!" cried Inglewood, turning round in a singular excitement. "There must be something to wake up to! All we do is preparations—your cleanliness, and my healthiness, and Warner's scientific appliances. We're always preparing for something—something that never comes off. I ventilate the house, and you sweep the house, but what is going to happen in the house?"

She was looking at him quietly, but with very bright eyes, and seemed to be searching for some form of words which she could not find.

Before she could speak, the door burst open, and the boisterous Rosamund Hunt, in her flamboyant white hat, boa, and parasol, stood framed in the doorway. She was in a breathing heat, and on her open face was an expression of the most infantile astonishment.

"Well, here's a fine game," she said, panting; "what am I to do now I wonder. I've wired for Dr. Warner, that's all I can think of doing."

"What is the matter?" asked Diana rather sharply, but moving forward, like one used to be called upon for assistance.

"It's Mary," said the heiress, "my companion, Mary Gray, that cracked friend of yours called Smith has proposed to her in the garden, after ten hours' acquaintance, and he wants to go off with her now for a special licence."

Arthur Inglewood walked to the open French windows and looked out on the garden, still golden with evening light. Nothing moved there but a bird or two hopping and twittering; but beyond the hedge and railings, in the road outside the garden gate, a hansom-cab was waiting, with the yellow Gladstone bag on top of it.

CHAPTER IV

THE GARDEN OF THE GOD

DIANA DUKE seemed inexplicably irritated at the abrupt entrance and utterance of the other girl.

"Well," she said shortly, "I suppose Miss Gray can decline him if she doesn't want to marry him."

"But she does want to marry him!" cried Rosamund in exasperation. "She's a wild, wicked fool, and I won't be parted from her."

"Perhaps," said Diana icily; "but I really don't see what we can do."

"But the man's balmy, Diana," reasoned her friend angrily. "I can't let my nice governess marry a man that's balmy! You or somebody must stop it! Mr. Inglewood, you're a man— go and tell them they simply can't."

"Unfortunately, it seems to me they simply can," said Inglewood, with a depressed air. "I have far less right of intervention than Miss Duke; besides having far less moral force than she."

"You haven't either of you got much," cried Rosamund, the last stays of her formidable temper giving way; "I think I'll go somewhere else for a little sense and pluck. I think I know some one who will help me more than you do, at any rate . . . he's a cantankerous beast, but he's a man and has a mind, and knows it. . . ." And she flung out into the garden, with cheeks aflame, and the parasol whirling like a Catharine wheel.

She found Michael Moon standing under the garden tree, looking over the hedge; hunched like a bird of prey, with his large pipe hanging down his long blue chin. The very hardness of his expression pleased her, after the nonsense of the new engagement, and the shilly-shallying of her other friends.

"I am sorry I was cross, Mr. Moon," she said frankly. "I hated you for being a cynic; but I've been well punished, for I want a cynic just now. I've had my fill of sentiment—I'm fed up with it. The world's gone mad, Mr. Moon—all except the cynics, I think. That maniac Smith wants to marry my old friend Mary, and she—and she—doesn't seem to mind."

Seeing his attentive face still undisturbedly smoking, she added smartly, "I'm not joking—that's Mr. Smith's cab outside. He swears he'll take her off now to his aunt's, and go for a special licence. Do give me some practical advice, Mr. Moon."

Mr. Moon took his pipe out of his mouth, held it in his hand for an instant reflectively, and then tossed it to the other side of the garden. "My practical advice to you is this," he said: "Let him go for his special licence, and ask him to get another one for you and me.

"Is that one of your jokes?" asked the young lady. "Do say what you really mean."

"I mean that Innocent Smith is a man of business," said Moon with ponderous precision. "A plain, practical man; a man of affairs; a man of facts and the daylight. He has let down twenty ton of good building bricks suddenly on my head, and I am glad to say they have woken me up. We went to sleep a little while ago on this very lawn, in this very sunlight. We have had a little nap for five years or so, but now we're going to be married, Rosamund, and I can't see why that cab. . . ."

"Really," said Rosamund stoutly, "I don't know what you mean."

"What a lie!" cried Michael, advancing on her with brightening eyes. "I'm all for lies in an ordinary way; but don't you see that tonight they won't do? We've wandered into a world of facts, old girl. That grass growing, and that sun going down, and that cab at the door, are facts. You used to torment and excuse yourself by saying I was after your money, and didn't really love you. But if I stood here now, and told you I didn't love you —you wouldn't believe me. For truth is in this garden to-night."

"Really, Mr. Moon . . ." said Rosamund, rather more faintly.

He kept two big blue magnetic eyes fixed on her face. "Is my name Moon?" he asked. "Is your name Hunt? On my honour, they sound to me as quaint and distant as Red Indian names. It's as if your name was 'Swim,' and my name was 'Sunrise.' But our real names are Husband and Wife, as they were when we fell asleep."

"It is no good," said Rosamund, with real tears in her eyes; "one can never go back."

"I can go where I damn please," said Michael, "and I can carry you on my shoulder."

"But really, Michael, really, you must stop and think!" cried the girl earnestly. "You could carry me off my feet I dare say, soul and body, but it may be bitter bad business for all that. These things done in that romantic rush, like Mr. Smith's, they—they do attract women, I don't deny it. As you say, we're all telling the truth to-night. They've attracted poor Mary, for one. They attract me, Michael. But the cold fact remains: imprudent marriages do lead to long unhappiness and disappointment—you've got used to your drinks and things—I shan't be pretty much longer—"

"Imprudent marriages 1" roared Michael. "And pray where in earth or heaven are there any prudent marriages? Might as well talk about prudent suicides. You and I have dawdled round each other long enough, and are we any safer than Smith and Mary Gray who met last night? You never know a husband till you marry him. Unhappy! Of course you'll be unhappy! Who the devil are you that you shouldn't be unhappy, like the mother that bore you? Disappointed I Of course we'll be disappointed! I, for one, don't expect till I die to be so good a man as I am at this minute, for just now I'm fifty thousand feet high, a tower with all the trumpets shouting."

"You see all this," said Rosamund, with a grand sincerity in her solid face, "and do you really want to marry me?"

"My darling, what else is there to do?" reasoned the Irishman. "What other occupation is there for an active man on this earth, except to marry you? What's the alternative to marriage, barring sleep? It's not liberty, Rosamund. Unless you marry God, as our nuns do in Ireland, you must marry Man; that is Me. The only third thing is to marry yourself—to live with yourself—yourself, yourself, yourself—the only companion that is never satisfied—and never satisfactory."

"Michael," said Miss Hunt, in a very soft voice, "if you won't talk so much, I'll marry you."

"It's no time for talking," cried Michael Moon. "Singing is the only thing. Can't you find that mandoline of yours, Rosamund."

"Go and fetch it for me," said Rosamund, with crisp and sharp authority.

The lounging Mr. Moon stood for one split second astonished, then he shot away across the lawn, as if shod with the feathered shoes out of the Greek fairy tale. He cleared three yards and fifteen daisies at a leap, out of mere bodily levity; but when he came within a yard or two of the open parlour windows, his flying feet fell in their old manner like lead; he twisted round and came back slowly, whistling. The events of that enchanted evening were not at an end.

Inside the dark sitting-room of which Moon had caught a glimpse, a curious thing had happened, almost an instant after the intemperate exit of Rosamund. It was something which, occurring in that obscure parlour, that seemed to Arthur Inglewood like heaven and earth turning head over heels, the sea being the ceiling and the stars the floor. No words can express how it astonished him, as it astonishes all simple men when it happens. Yet the stiffest female stoicism seems separated from it, only by a sheet of paper or a sheet of steel. It indicates no surrender, far less any sympathy. The most rigid and ruthless woman can begin to cry, just as the most effeminate man can grow a beard. It is a separate sexual power, and proves nothing one way or the other about force of character. But to young men ignorant of women, like Arthur Inglewood, to see Diana Duke crying was like seeing a motorcar shedding tears of oil.

He could never have given (even if his really manly modesty had permitted it) any vaguest vision of what he did when he saw that portent. He acted as men do when a theatre catches fire—very differently from what they would have conceived themselves as acting, whether for better or worse. He had a faint memory of certain half-stifled explanations, that the heiress was the one really paying guest, and she would go, and the bailiffs (in consequence) would come; but after that he knew nothing of his own conduct except by the protests it evoked.

"Leave me alone, Mr. Inglewood—leave me alone—that's not the way to help."

"But I can help you," said Arthur, with grinding certainty; "I can, I can, I can. . . ."

"Why, you said," cried the girl, "that you were much weaker than me."

"So I am weaker than you," said Arthur, in a voice that went vibrating through everything, "but not just now."

"Let go my hands!" cried Diana. "I won't be bullied."

In one element he was much stronger than she, the matter of humour. This leapt up in him suddenly and he laughed, saying: "Well, you are mean. You know quite well you'll bully me all the rest of my life. You might allow a man the one minute of his life when he's allowed to bully."

It was as extraordinary for him to laugh as for her to cry; and for the first time since her childhood Diana was entirely off her guard.

"Do you mean you want to marry me?" she said.

"Why, there's a cab at the door!" cried Inglewood, springing up with an unconscious energy and bursting open the glass doors that led into the garden,

As he led her out by the hand they realized somehow for the first time that the house and garden were on a steep height over London. And yet, though they felt the place to be uplifted, they felt it also to be secret: it was like some round-walled garden on the top of one of the turrets of heaven.

Inglewood looked around dreamily, his brown eyes devouring all sorts of details with a senseless delight. He noticed for the first time that the railings of the gate beyond the garden bushes were moulded like little spearheads, and painted blue. He noticed that one of the blue spears was loosened in its place, and hung sideways; and this almost made him laugh. He thought it somehow exquisitely harmless and funny that the railing should be crooked; he thought he should like to know how it happened; who did it; and how the man was getting on.

When they were gone a few feet across that fiery grass they realized that they were not alone. Rosamund Hunt and the eccentric Mr. Moon, both of whom they had last seen in the blackest temper of detachment, were standing together on the lawn. They were standing in quite an ordinary manner, and yet they looked somehow like people in a book.

"Oh!" said Diana. "What lovely air!"

"I know," called out Rosamund, with a pleasure so positive that it rang out like a complaint. "It's just like that horrid, beastly, fizzy stuff they gave me that made me feel happy."

"Oh, it isn't like anything but itself!" answered Diana, breathing deeply. "Why, it's all cold, and yet it feels like fire."

"Balmy is the word we use in Fleet Street," said Mr. Moon. "Balmy—especially on the crumpet." And he fanned himself quite unnecessarily with his straw hat. They were all full of little leaps and pulsations of objectless and airy energy. Diana stirred and stretched her long arms rigidly, as if crucified, in a sort of excruciating restfulness; Michael stood still for long intervals, with gathered muscles, then spun round like a teetotum, and stood still again; Rosamund did not trip, for women never trip, except when they fall on their noses, but she struck the ground with her foot as she moved, as if to some inaudible dance tune; and Inglewood, leaning quite quietly against a tree, had unconsciously clutched a branch and shaken it with a creative violence. Those giant gestures of man, that make the high statues and the strokes of war, tossed and tormented all their limbs. Silently as they strolled and stood they were bursting like batteries with an animal magnetism.

"And now," cried Moon quite suddenly, stretching out a hand on each side, "let's dance round that bush!"

"Why, what bush do you mean?" asked Rosamund, looking round with a sort of radiant rudeness.

"The bush that isn't there," said Michael; "the Mulberry Bush."

They had taken each other's hands, half laughing and quite ritually; and before they could disconnect again Michael spun them all round, like a demon spinning the world for a top. Diana felt, as the circle of the horizon flew instantaneously around her, a far aerial sense of the ring of heights beyond London and corners where she had climbed as a child; she seemed almost to hear the rooks cawing about the old pines on Highgate, or to see the glow-worms gathering and kindling in the woods of Box Hill.

The circle broke—as all such perfect circles of levity must break—and sent its author, Michael, flying as by centrifugal force, far away against the blue rails of the gate. When reeling there, he suddenly raised shout after shout of a new and quite dramatic character.

"Why, it's Warner!" he shouted, waving his arms. "It's jolly old Warner—with a new silk hat and the old silk moustache!"

"Is that Dr. Warner?" cried Rosamund, bounding forward in a burst of memory, amusement, and distress. "Oh, I'm so sorry! Oh, do tell him it's all right!"

"Let's take hands and tell him," said Michael Moon. For, indeed, while they were talking, another hansom had dashed up behind the one already waiting, and Dr. Herbert Warner, leaving a companion in the cab, had carefully deposited himself on the pavement.

Now, when you are an eminent physician and are wired for by an heiress to come to a case of dangerous mania, and when, as you come in through the garden to the house, the heiress and her landlady and two of the gentlemen boarders join hands and dance round you in a ring, calling out, "It's all right! it's all right!" you are apt to be flustered, and even displeased. Dr. Warner was a placid but hardly a placable person. The two things are by no means the same; and even when Moon explained to him that he, Warner, with his high hat and tall, solid figure, was just such a classic column as ought to be danced round by a ring of laughing maidens on some old golden Greek seashore— even then he seemed to miss the point of the general rejoicing.

"Inglewood!" cried Dr. Warner, fixing his former disciple with a stare, "are you mad?"

Arthur flushed to the roots of his brown hair, but he answered easily and quietly enough, "Not now. The truth is, Warner, I've just made a rather important medical discovery— quite in your line."

"What do you mean?" asked the great doctor stiffly. "What discovery?"

"I've discovered that health really is catching, like disease," answered Arthur.

"Yes; sanity has broken out, and is spreading," said Michael, performing a pas seul with a thoughtful expression. "Twenty thousand more cases taken to the hospitals: nurses employed night and day."

Dr. Warner studied Michael's grave face and lightly moving legs with an unfathomed wonder. "And is this, may I ask," he said, "the sanity that is spreading?"

"You must forgive me, Dr. Warner," cried Rosamund Hunt heartily. "I know I've treated you badly; but indeed it was all a mistake. I was in a frightfully bad temper when I sent for you, but now it all seems like a dream—and—and Mr. Smith is the sweetest, most sensible, most delightful old thing that ever existed, and he may marry any one he likes—except me."

"I should suggest Mrs. Duke," said Michael.

The gravity of Dr. Warner's face increased. He took a slip of pink paper from his waistcoat pocket, with his pale blue eyes quietly fixed on Rosamund's face all the time. He spoke with a not inexcusable frigidity.

"Really, Miss Hunt," he said, "you are not yet very reassuring. You sent me this wire only half an hour ago—'Come at once, if possible, with another doctor. Man—Innocent Smith—gone mad on premises, and doing dreadful things. Do you know anything of him?' I went round at once to a distinguished colleague of mine, a doctor who is also a private detective and an authority on criminal lunacy; he has come round with me, and is waiting in the cab. Now you calmly tell me that this criminal madman is a highly sweet and sane old thing, with accompaniments that set me speculating on your own definitions of sanity. I hardly comprehend the change."

"Oh, how can one explain a change in sun and moon and everybody's soul?" cried Rosamund, in despair. "Must I confess we had got so morbid as to think him mad, merely because he wanted to get married? And that we didn't even know it was only because we wanted to get married ourselves? We'll humiliate ourselves, if you like, doctor; we're happy enough."

"Where is Mr. Smith?" asked Warner of Inglewood very sharply.

Arthur started; he had forgotten all about the central figure of their farce, who had not been visible for an hour or more.

"I—I think he's on the other side of the house, by the dustbin," he said.

"He may be on the road to Russia," said Warner; "but he must be found." And he strode away and disappeared round a corner of the house by the sunflowers.

"I hope," said Rosamund, "he won't really interfere with Mr. Smith."

"Interfere with the daisies!" said Michael with a snort. "A man can't be locked up for falling in love—at least, I hope not."

"No, I think even a doctor couldn't make a disease out of him. He'd throw off the doctor like the disease, don't you know. I believe it's a case of a sort of saint. I believe Innocent Smith is simply innocent, and that is why he is so extraordinary."

It was Rosamund who spoke, restlessly tracing circles in the grass with the point of her white shoe.

"I think," said Inglewood, "that Smith is not extraordinary at all. He's comic just because he's so startlingly commonplace. Don't you know what it is to be in all one family circle, with aunts and uncles, when a schoolboy comes home for the holidays? That bag there on the cab is only a schoolboy's hamper. This tree here in the garden is only the sort of tree that any schoolboy would have climbed. Yes, that's the thing that has haunted us all about him, the thing we could never fit a word to. Whether he is my old schoolfellow or no, at least he is all my old schoolfellows. He is the endless bun-eating, ball-throwing animal that we have all been."

"That is only you absurd boys," said Diana. "I don't believe any girl was ever so silly, and I'm sure no girl was ever so happy; except—" and she stopped.

"I will tell you the truth about Innocent Smith," said Michael Moon in a low voice. "Dr. Warner has gone to look for him in vain. He is not there. Haven't you noticed that we never saw him since we found ourselves? He was an astral baby born of all four of us; he was only our own youth returned. Long before poor old Warner had clambered out of his cab, the thing we called Smith had dissolved into dew and light on this lawn. Once or twice more, by the mercy of God, we may feel the thing, but the man we shall never see. In a spring garden before breakfast we shall smell the smell called Smith. In the snapping of brisk twigs in tiny fires we shall hear a noise named Smith. Everything insatiable and innocent in the grasses that gobble up the earth like babies at a bun feast, in the white mornings that split the sky as a boy splits up white fir-wood, we may feel for one instant the presence of an impetuous purity; but his innocence was too close to the unconsciousness of inanimate things not to melt back at a mere touch into the mild hedges and heavens; he—"

He was interrupted from behind the house by a bang like that of a bomb. Almost at the same instant the stranger in the cab sprang out of it, leaving it rocking upon the stones of the road. He clutched the blue railings of the garden, and peered eagerly over them in the direction of the noise. He was a small, loose yet alert man, very thin, with a face that seemed made out of fish bones, and a silk hat quite as rigid and resplendent as Warner's, but thrust back recklessly on the hinder part of his head.

"Murder!" he shrieked, in a high and feminine but very penetrating voice. "Stop that murderer there!"

Even as he shrieked a second shot shook the lower windows of the house, and with the noise of it Dr. Herbert Warner came flying round the corner like a leaping rabbit. Yet before he had reached the group a third discharge had deafened them; and they saw with their own eyes two spots of white sky drilled through the second of the unhappy Herbert's high hats. The next moment the fugitive physician fell over a flowerpot, and came down on all fours, staring like a cow. The hat with the two shot-holes in it rolled upon the gravel path before him, and Innocent Smith came round the corner like a railway-train. He was looking twice his proper size —a giant clad in green, the big revolver still smoking in his hand, his face sanguine and in shadow, his eyes blazing like stars, and his yellow hair standing out all ways like Struwel-peter's.

Though this startling scene hung but an instant in stillness, Inglewood had time to feel once more what he had felt when he saw the other lovers standing on the lawn; the sensation of a certain cut and coloured clearness that belongs rather to the things of art than to the things of experience. The broken flowerpot with its red-hot geraniums, the green bulk of Smith and the black bulk of Warner, the blue-spiked railings behind, clutched by the stranger's yellow vulture claws and peered over by his long vulture neck, the silk hat on the gravel, and the little cloudlet of smoke floating across the garden as innocently as the puff of a cigarette: all these seemed unnaturally distinct and definite. They existed, like symbols, in an ecstasy of separation. Indeed, every object grew more and more particular and precious because the whole picture was breaking up. Things look so bright just before they burst.

Long before his fancies had begun, let alone ceased, Arthur had stepped across and taken one of Smith's arms. Simultaneously the little stranger had run up the steps and taken the other. Smith went into peals of laughter, and surrendered his pistol with perfect willingness. Moon raised the doctor to his feet, and then went and leaned sullenly on the garden gate. The girls were quiet and vigilant, as good women mostly are in instants of catastrophe, but their faces showed that somehow or other a light had been dashed out of their sky. The doctor himself, when he had risen, collected his hat and wits, and dusted himself down with an air of great disgust, turned to them in brief apology. He was very white with his recent panic, but he spoke with perfect self-control.

"You will excuse us, ladies," he said, "my friend and Mr. Inglewood are both scientists in their several ways; I think we had better all take Mr. Smith indoors, and communicate with you later."

And under the guard of the three natural philosophers, the disarmed Smith was led tactfully into the house, still roaring with laughter.

From time to time during the next twenty minutes his distant boom of mirth could again be heard through the half-open window; but there came no echo of the quiet voices of the physicians. The girls walked about the garden together, rubbing up each other's spirits as best they might; Michael Moon still hung heavily against the gate. Somewhere about the expiration of that time, Dr. Warner came out of the house again with a face less pale but even more stern, and the little man with the fish-bone face advanced gravely in his rear. And if the face of Warner in the sunlight was that of a hanging judge, the face of the little man behind was more like a death's head.

"Miss Hunt," said Dr. Herbert Warner, "I only wish to offer you my warm thanks and admiration. By your prompt courage and wisdom in sending for us by wire this evening, you have enabled us to capture and put out of mischief one of the most cruel and terrible of the enemies of humanity; a criminal whose plausibility and pitilessness have never been before combined in flesh."

Rosamund looked across at him with a white, blank face and blinking eyes. "What do you mean?" she asked. "You can't mean Mr. Smith?"

"He has gone by many other names," said the doctor gravely. "And not one he did not leave to be cursed behind him. That man, Miss Hunt, has left a track of blood and tears across the world. Whether he is mad as well as wicked, we are trying, in the interests of science, to discover. In any case, we shall have to take him before a magistrate first, even if only on the road to a lunatic asylum. But the lunatic asylum in which he is confined will have to be sealed with wall within wall, and ringed with guns like a fortress, or he will break out again to bring forth carnage and darkness on the earth."

Rosamund looked at the two doctors, her face growing paler and paler; then her eyes strayed to Michael who was leaning on the gate, but he continued to lean on it without moving, with his face turned away towards the darkening road.

## CHAPTER V

## THE ALLEGORICAL PRACTICAL JOKER

THE criminal specialist who had come with Dr. Warner was a somewhat more urbane and even dapper figure, on closer inspection, than he had appeared when clutching the railings and craning his neck into the garden. He even looked comparatively young when he took his hat off, having fair hair parted in the middle and carefully curled on each side, and lively movements especially of the hands. He had a dandified monocle slung round his neck by a broad black ribbon, and a big bow tie, as if a big American moth had alighted on him. His dress and gestures were bright enough for a boy's; it was only when you looked at the fish-bone face itself that you beheld something acrid and old. His manners were excellent, though hardly English, and he had two half-conscious tricks by which people who only met him once remembered him. One was a trick of closing his eyes when he wished to be particularly polite; the other was one of lifting his joined thumb and forefinger in the air as if holding a pinch of snuff, when he was hesitating or hovering over a word. But those who were longer in his company tended to forget these oddities in the stream of his quaint and solemn conversation, and really singular views.

"Miss Hunt," said Dr. Warner, "this is Dr. Cyrus Pym."

Dr. Cyrus Pym shut his eyes during the introduction, rather as if he were "playing fair" in some child's game; and gave a prompt little bow which somehow suddenly revealed him as a citizen of the United States.

"Dr. Cyrus Pym," continued Warner (Dr. Pym shut his eyes again), "is perhaps the first criminological expert of America. We are very fortunate to be able to consult with him in this extraordinary case—"

"I can't make head or tail of anything," said Rosamund. "How can poor Mr. Smith be so dreadful as he is by your account?"

"Or by your telegram," said Herbert Warner, smiling.

"Oh, you don't understand," cried the girl impatiently. "Why, he's done us, all more good than going to church."

"I think I can explain to the young lady," said Dr. Cyrus Pym. "This criminal or maniac Smith is a very genius of evil and has a method of his own, a method of the most daring ingenuity. He is popular wherever he goes, for he invades every house as an uproarious child. People are getting suspicious of all the respectable disguises for a scoundrel; so he always uses the disguise of—what shall I say—the Bohemian, the blameless Bohemian. He always carries people off their feet. People are used to the mask of conventional good conduct. He goes in for eccentric goodnature. You expect a Don Juan to dress up as a solemn and solid Spanish merchant; but you're not prepared for Don Juan when he dresses up as Don Quixote. You expect a humbug to behave like Sir Charles Grandi-son; because (with all respect, Miss Hunt, for the deep, tear-moving tenderness of Samuel Richardson) Sir Charles Grandison so often behaved like a humbug. But no real red-blooded citizen is quite ready for a humbug that models himself not on Sir Charles Grandi-son but on Sir Roger de Coverley. Setting up to be a good man a little cracked is a new criminal incognito, Miss Hunt. It's been a great notion, and commonly successful; but its success just makes it mighty cruel. I can forgive Dick Turpin if he impersonates Dr. Busby; I can't forgive him when he impersonates Dr. Johnson. The saint with a tile loose is a bit too sacred, I guess, to be parodied."

"But how do you know," cried Rosamund desperately, "that Mr. Smith is a known criminal?"

"I collated all the documents," said the American, "when my friend Warner knocked me up on receipt of your cable. It is my professional affair to know these facts, Miss Hunt; and there's no more doubt about them than about the Bradshaw down at the depot. This man has hitherto escaped the law, through his admirable affectations of infancy or insanity. But I myself, as a specialist, have privately authenticated notes of some eighteen or twenty crimes attempted or achieved in this manner. He comes to houses as he has to this, and gets a grand popularity. He makes things go. They do go; when he's gone the things are gone. Gone, Miss Hunt, gone, a man's life or a man's spoons, or more often a woman. I assure you, I have all the memoranda."

"I have seen them," said Warner solidly. "I can assure you this is all correct."

"The most unmanly aspect, according to my feelings," went on the American doctor, "is this perpetual deception of innocent women by a wild simulation of innocence. From almost every house where this great imaginative devil has been, he has taken some poor girl away with him; some say he's got a hypnotic eye with his other queer features, and that they go like automata. What's become of all those poor girls nobody knows. Murdered, I dare say; for we've lots of instances, besides this one, of his turning his hand to murder, though none ever brought him under the law. Anyhow, our most modern methods of research can't find any trace of the wretched women. It's when I think of them that I am real moved, Miss Hunt. And I've really nothing else to say just now except what Dr. Warner has said."

"Quite so," said Warner, with a smile that seemed moulded in marble; "that we all have to thank you very much for that telegram."

The little Yankee scientist had been speaking with such evident sincerity that one forgot the tricks of his voice and manner, the falling eyelids, the rising intonation, and the poised finger and thumb, which were at other times a little comic. It was not so much that he was cleverer than Warner; perhaps he was not so clever, though he was more celebrated. But he had what Warner never had, a fresh and unaffected seriousness; the great American virtue of simplicity. Rosamund knitted her brows and looked gloomily towards the darkening house that contained the dark prodigy.

Broad daylight still endured; but it had already changed from gold to silver, and was changing from silver to gray. The long plumy shadows of the one or two trees in the garden faded more and more upon a dead background of dusk. In the sharpest and

deepest shadow, which was the entrance to the house by the big French windows, Rosamund could watch a hurried consultation between Inglewood (who was still left in charge of the mysterious captive) and Diana, who had moved to his assistance from without. After a few sentences and gestures they went inside, shutting the glass doors upon the garden; and the garden seemed to grow grayer still.

The American gentleman named Pym seemed to be turning and on the move in the same direction; but before he started he spoke to Rosamund, with a flash of that guileless tact which redeemed much of his childish vanity, and with something of that spontaneous poetry which made it difficult, pedantic as he was, to call him a pedant.

"I'm vurry sorry, Miss Hunt," he said, "but Dr. Warner and I, as two qual'i-fied practitioners, had better take Mr. Smith away in that cab, and the less said about it the better. Don't you agitate yourself, Miss Hunt. YouVe just got to think that we're taking away a monstrosity, something that oughtn't to be at all. Something like one of those gods in your Britannic Museum, all wings, and beards, and legs, and eyes, and no shape. That's what Smith is, and you shall soon be quit of him."

He had already taken a step towards the house and Warner was about to follow him, when the glass doors were opened again and Diana Duke came out with more than her usual quickness across the lawn. Her face was aquiver with worry and excitement, and her dark earnest eyes fixed only on the other girl.

"Rosamund," she cried in despair, "what shall I do with her?"

"With her?" cried Miss Hunt, with a violent jump. "O lord, he isn't a woman, too, is he?"

"No, no, no," said Dr. Pym soothingly, as if in common fairness. "A woman, no, really, he is not so bad as that."

"I mean your friend Mary Gray," retorted Diana with equal tartness. "What on earth am I to do with her?"

"How can we tell her about Smith, you mean," answered Rosamund, her face at once clouding and softening. "Yes, it will be pretty painful."

"But I have told her," exploded Diana, with more than her congenital exasperation. "I have told her and she doesn't seem to mind. She still says she's going away with Smith in that cab."

"But it's impossible!" ejaculated Rosamund. "Why, Mary is really religious. She—"

She stopped in time to realize that Mary Gray was comparatively close to her on the lawn. Her quiet companion had come down very quietly into the garden, but dressed very decisively for travel. She had a neat but very ancient blue-gray Tam o' Shanter on her head, and was pulling some rather threadbare gray gloves on to her hands. Yet the two tints fitted excellently with her heavy copper-coloured hair; the more excellently for the touch of shabbiness: for a woman's clothes never suit her so well as when they seem to suit her by accident.

But in this case the woman had a quality yet more unique and attractive. In such gray hours, when the sun is sunk and the skies are already sad, it will often happen that one reflection at some occasional angle will cause to linger the last of the light. A scrap of window, a scrap of water, a scrap of looking-glass, will be full of the fire that is lost to all the rest of the earth. The quaint, almost triangular face of Mary Gray was like some triangular piece of mirror that could still repeat the splendour of hours before. Mary, though she was always graceful, could never have properly been called beautiful; and yet her happiness amid all that misery was so beautiful as to make a man catch his breath.

"O Diana," cried Rosamund in a lower voice and altering her phrase; "but how did you tell her?"

"It is quite easy to tell her," answered Diana sombrely; "it makes no impression at all."

"I'm afraid I've kept everything waiting," said Mary Gray apologetically, "and now we must really say good-bye. Innocent is taking me to his aunt's over at Hampstead, and I'm afraid she goes to bed early."

Her words were quite casual and practical, but there was a sort of sleepy light in her eyes that was more baffling than darkness; she was like one speaking absently with her eye on some very distant object.

"Mary, Mary," cried Rosamund, almost breaking down; "I'm so sorry about it, but the thing can't be at all. We—we have found out all about Mr. Smith."

"All?" repeated Mary, with a low and curious intonation; "why, that must be awfully exciting."

There was no noise for an instant and no motion except that the silent Michael Moon, leaning on the gate, lifted his head, as it might be to listen. Then Rosamund remaining speechless, Dr. Pym came to her rescue in his definite way.

"To begin with," he said, "this man Smith is constantly attempting murder. The Warden of Brakespeare College—"

"I know," said Mary, with a vague but radiant smile; "Innocent told me."

"I can't say what he told you," replied Pym quickly, "but I'm very much afraid it wasn't true. The plain truth is that the man's stained with every known human crime. I assure you, I have all the documents. I have evidence of his committing burglary, signed by a most eminent English curate. I have—"

"Oh, but there were two curates," cried Mary, with a certain gentle eagerness, "that was what made it so much funnier."

The darkened glass doors of the house opened once more and Inglewood appeared for an instant, making a sort of signal. The American doctor bowed, the English doctor did not, but they both set out stolidly towards the house. No one else moved, not even Michael hanging on the gate; but the back of his head and shoulders had still an indescribable indication that he was listening to every word.

"But don't you understand, Mary," cried Rosamund in despair; "don't you know that awful things have happened even before our very eyes. I should have thought you would have heard the revolver shots upstairs."

"Yes, I heard the shots," said Mary almost brightly; "but I was busy packing just then. And Innocent had told me he was going to shoot at Dr. Warner; so it wasn't worth while to come down."

"Oh, I don't understand what you mean," cried Rosamund Hunt, stamping, "but you must and shall understand what I mean. I don't care how cruelly I put it, if only I can save you. I mean that your Innocent Smith is the most awfully wicked man in the world. He has sent bullets at lots of other men and gone off in cabs with lots of other women. And he seems to have killed the women, too, for nobody can find them."

"He is really rather naughty sometimes," said Mary Gray, laughing softly as she buttoned her old gray gloves.

"Oh, this is really mesmerism, or something," said Rosamund, and burst into tears.

At the same moment the two black-clad doctors appeared out of the house with their great green-clad captive between them. He made no resistance, but was still laughing in a groggy and half-witted style. Arthur Ingle-wood followed in the rear, a dark and red study in the last shades of distress and shame. In this black, funereal, and painfully realistic style the exit from Beacon House was made by the man whose entrance a day before had been effected by the happy leaping of a wall

and the hilarious climbing of a tree. No one moved of the groups in the garden except Mary Gray, who stepped forward quite naturally, calling out, "Are you ready, Innocent? Our cab's been waiting such a long time."

"Ladies and gentlemen," said Dr. Warner firmly, "I must insist on asking this lady to stand aside. We shall have trouble enough as it is, with the three of us in a cab."

"But it is our cab," persisted Mary. "Why, there's Innocent's yellow bag on the top of it."

"Stand aside," repeated Warner roughly. "And you, Mr. Moon, please be so obliging as to move a moment. Come, come! the sooner this ugly business is over the better— and how can we open the gate if you will keep leaning on it?"

Michael Moon looked at his long lean forefinger, and seemed to consider and reconsider this argument. "Yes," he said at last; "but how can I lean on this gate if you keep on opening it?"

"Oh, get out of the way!" cried Warner, almost good-humouredly. "You can lean on the gate any time."

"No," said Moon reflectively. "Seldom the time and the place and the old gate altogether; and it all depends whether you come of an old country family. My ancestors leaned on gates before any one had discovered how to open them."

"Michael!" cried Arthur Inglewood in a kind of agony, "are you going to get out of the way?"

"Why, no; I think not," said Michael, after some meditation, and swung himself slowly round, so that he confronted the company, while still, in a lounging attitude, occupying the path.

"Hullo!" he called out suddenly; "what are you doing to Mr. Smith?"

"Taking him away," answered Warner shortly, "to be examined."

"Matriculation?" asked Moon brightly.

"By a magistrate," said the other curtly.

"And what other magistrate," cried Michael, raising his voice, "dares to try what befell on this free soil, save only the ancient and independent dukes of Beacon? What other court dares to try one of our company, save only the High Court of Beacon? Have you forgotten that only this afternoon we flew the flag of independence and severed ourselves from all the nations of the earth?"

"Michael," cried Rosamund, wringing her hands, "how can you stand there talking nonsense? Why, you saw the dreadful thing yourself. You were there when he went mad. It was you that helped the doctor up when he fell over the flowerpot."

"And the High Court of Beacon," replied Moon with hauteur, "has special powers in all cases concerning lunatics, flowerpots, and doctors who fall down in gardens. It's in our very first charter from Edward I: 'Si med-icus quisquam in horto prostratus' "

"Out of the way!" cried Warner with sudden fury, "or we will force you out of it."

"What!" cried Michael Moon, with a cry of hilarious fierceness. "Shall I die in defence of this sacred pale? Will you paint these blue railings red with my gore?" and he laid hold of one of the blue spikes behind him. As Arthur Inglewood had noticed earlier in the evening, the railing was loose and crooked at this place, and the painted iron staff and no

spear-head came away in Michael's hand as he shook it.

"See!" he cried, brandishing this broken javelin in the air, "the very lances round Beacon Tower leap from their places to defend it. Ah, in such a place and hour it is a fine thing to die alone!" And in a voice like a drum he rolled the noble lines of Ron-sard—

"Ou pour l'honneur de Dieu, ou pour le droit de mon prince, Navre, poitrine ouverte, au bord de mon province."

"Sakes alive!" said the American gentleman, almost in an awed tone. Then he added, "Are there two maniacs here?"

"No; there are five," thundered Moon. "Smith and I are the only sane people left."

"Michael!" cried Rosamund; "Michael, what does it mean?"

"It means bosh!" roared Michael, and slung his painted spear hurtling to the other end of the garden. "It means that doctors are bosh, and criminology is bosh, and Americans are bosh—much more bosh than our Court of Beacon. It means, you fat-heads, in

that Innocent Smith is no more mad or bad than the bird on that tree."

"But, my dear Moon," began Inglewood in his modest manner, "these gentlemen—"

"On the word of two doctors," exploded Moon again, without listening to anybody else, "shut up in a private hell on the word of two doctors! And such doctors! Oh, my hat! Look at 'em!—do just look at 'em! Would you read a book, or buy a dog, or go to a hotel on the advice of twenty such? My people came from Ireland, and were Catholics. What would you say if I called a man wicked on the word of two priests?"

"But it isn't only their word, Michael," reasoned Rosamund; "they've got evidence too."

"Have you looked at it?" asked Moon.

"No," said Rosamund, with a sort of faint surprise; "these gentlemen are in charge of it."

"And of everything else, it seems to me," said Michael. "Why, you haven't even had the decency to consult Mrs. Duke."

"Oh, that's no use," said Diana in an undertone to Rosamund; "auntie couldn't say 'Bo!' to a goose."

"I am glad to hear it," answered Michael, a for with such a flock of geese to say it to, the horrid expletive might be constantly on her lips. For my part, I simply refuse to let things be done in this light and airy style. I appeal to Mrs. Duke—it's her house."

"Mrs. Duke?" repeated Inglewood doubtfully.

"Yes, Mrs. Duke," said Michael firmly, "commonly called the Iron Duke."

"If you ask auntie," said Diana quietly, "she'll only be for doing nothing at all. Her only idea is to hush things up or to let things slide. That just suits her."

"Yes," replied Michael Moon; "and, as it happens, it just suits all of us. You are impatient with your elders, Miss Duke; but when you are as old yourself you will know what Napoleon knew—that half one's letters answer themselves if you can only refrain from the fleshly appetite of answering them."

He was still lounging in the same absurd attitude, with his elbow on the gate, but his voice had altered abruptly for the third time; just as it had changed from the mock heroic to the humanly indignant, it now changed to the airy incisiveness of a lawyer giving good legal advice.

"It isn't only your aunt who wants to keep this quiet if she can," he said; "we all want to keep it quiet if we can. Look at the large facts—the big bones of the case. I believe these scientific gentlemen have made a highly scientific mistake. I believe Smith is as blameless as a buttercup. I admit buttercups don't often let off loaded pistols in private houses; I admit there is something demanding explanation. But I am morally certain there's some blunder, or some joke, or some allegory, or some accident behind all this. Well, suppose I'm wrong. We've disarmed him; we're five men to hold him; he may as well go to a lock-up later on as now. But suppose there's even a chance of my being right. Is it anybody's interest here to wash this linen in public?"

"Come, I'll take each of you in order. Once take Smith outside that gate, and you take him into the front page of the evening papers. I know; I've written the front page myself. Miss Duke, do you or your aunt want a sort of notice stuck up over your boarding-house—'Doctors shot here'? No, no— doctors are rubbish, as I said; but you don't want the rubbish shot here. Arthur, suppose I am right, or suppose I am wrong. Smith has appeared as an old schoolfellow of yours. Mark my words, if he's proved guilty, the Organs of Public Opinion will say you introduced him. If he's proved innocent, they will say you helped to collar him. Rosamund, my dear, suppose I am right or wrong. If he's proved guilty, they'll say you engaged your companion to him. If he's proved innocent, they'll print that telegram. I know the Organs, damn them."

He stopped an instant; for this rapid rationalism left him more breathless than had either his theatrical or his real denunciation. But he was plainly in earnest, as well as positive and lucid; as was proved by his proceeding quickly the moment he had found his breath.

"It is just the same," he cried, "with our medical friends. You will say that Dr. Warner has a grievance. I agree. But does he want specially to be snapshotted by all the journalists prostratus in horto? It was no fault of his, but the scene was not very dignified even for him. He must have justice; but does he want to ask for justice, not only on his knees but on his hands and knees? Does he want to enter the court of justice on all fours? Doctors are not allowed to advertise; and I'm sure no doctor wants to advertise himself as looking like that. And even for our American guest, the interest is the same. Let us suppose that he has conclusive documents. Let us assume that he has revelations really worth reading. Well, in a legal inquiry (or a medical inquiry, on that matter) ten to one he won't be allowed to read them. He'll be tripped up every two or three minutes with some tangle of old rules. A man can't tell the truth in public nowadays. But he can still tell it in private; he can tell it inside that house."

"It is quite true," said Dr. Cyrus Pym, who had listened throughout the speech with a seriousness which only an American could have retained through such a scene. "It is quite true that I have been perceptibly less hampered in private inquiries."

"Dr. Pym!" cried Warner in a sort of sudden anger. "Dr. Pym! you aren't surely going to admit—"

"Smith may be mad," went on the melancholy Moon in a monologue that seemed as heavy as a hatchet, "but there was something after all in what he said about Home Rule for every home. Yes, there is something, when all's said and done, in the High Court of Beacon. It is really true that human beings might often get some sort of domestic justice where just now they can only get legal injustice—oh, I am a lawyer, too, and I know that as well. It is true that there's too much official and indirect power. Often and often the thing a whole nation can't settle is just the thing a family could settle. Scores of young criminals have been fined and sent to jail when they ought to have been thrashed and sent to bed. Scores of men, I am sure have had a lifetime at Hanwell when they only wanted a week at Brighton. There is something in Smith's notion of domestic self-government; and I propose that we put it in practice. You have the prisoner, you have the documents. Come, we are a company of free, white, Christian people, such as might be besieged in a town or cast up on a desert island. Let us do this thing ourselves. Let us go into that house there and sit down and find out with our own eyes and ears whether this thing is true or not; whether this Smith is a man or a monster. If we can't do a little thing like that, what right have we to put crosses on ballot papers?"

Inglewood and Pym exchanged a glance; and Warner, who was no fool, saw in that glance that Moon was gaining ground. The motives that led Arthur to think of surrender were indeed very different from those which affected Dr. Cyrus Pym. All Arthur's instincts were on the side of privacy and a polite settlement; he was very English and would often endure wrongs rather than right them by scenes and serious rhetoric. To play at once the buffoon and the knight-errant, like his Irish friend, would have been absolute torture to him; but even the semi-official part he had played that afternoon was very painful. He was not likely to be reluctant if any one could convince him that his duty was to let sleeping dogs lie.

On the other hand, Cyrus Pym belonged to a country in which things are possible that seem crazy to the English. Regulations and authorities exactly like one of Innocent's pranks or one of Michael's satires really exist, propped by placid policemen and imposed on bustling business men. Pym knew whole states which are vast and yet secret and fanciful; each is as big as a nation yet as private as a lost village, and as unexpected as an apple-pie bed. States where no man may have a cigarette, states where any man may have ten wives, very strict prohibition states, very lax divorce states, all these large local vagaries had prepared Cyrus Pym's mind for small local vagaries in a smaller country. Infinitely more remote from England than any Russian or Italian, utterly incapable even of conceiving what English conventions are, he could not see the social impossibility of the Court of Beacon. It is firmly believed by those who shared the experiment, that to the very end Pym believed in that fantasmal court and believed it to be some Britannic institution.

Towards the synod thus somewhat at a standstill there approached through the growing haze and gloaming a short dark figure with a walk apparently founded on the imperfect repression of a negro breakdown; something at once in the familiarity and the incongruity of this being moved Michael to even heartier outbursts of a healthy and humane flippancy.

"Why, here's little Nosey Gould," he exclaimed. "Isn't the mere sight of him enough to banish all your morbid reflections?"

"Really," replied Dr. Warner, "I really fail to see how Mr. Gould affects the question; and I once more demand—"

"Hello! what's the funeral, gents?" inquired the newcomer with the air of an uproarious umpire. "Doctor demandin' something? Always the way at a boarding-house, you know. Always lots of demand. No supply."

As delicately and impartially as he could, Michael restated his position, and indicated generally that Smith had been guilty of certain dangerous and dubious acts and that there had even arisen an allegation that he was insane.

"Well, of course he is," said Moses Gould equably; "it don't need old 'Olmes to see that. The 'awk-like face of 'Omes," he added with abstract relish, "showed a shide of disappointment, the sleuth-like Gould 'avin' got there before 'im."

"If he is mad," began Inglewood.

"Well," said Moses, "when a cove gets out on the tiles the first night, there's generally a tile loose."

"You never objected before," said Diana Duke rather stiffly, "and you're generally pretty free with your complaints."

"I don't compline of him," said Moses magnanimously, "the poor chap's 'armless enough; you might tie 'im up in the garden here and 'e'd make noises at the buglars."

"Moses," said Moon with solemn fervour. "You are the incarnation of Common Sense. You think Mr. Innocent is mad. Let me introduce you to the incarnation of Scientific Theory. He also thinks Mr. Innocent is mad. Doctor, this is my friend Mr. Gould. Moses, this is the celebrated Dr. Cyrus Pym." The celebrated Dr. Cyrus Pym closed his eyes and bowed. He also murmured his national war-cry in a low voice, which sounded like, "Pleased to meet you."

"Now you two people," said Michael cheerfully, "who both think our poor friend mad, shall jolly well go into that house over there and prove him mad. What could be more powerful than the combination of Scientific Theory with Common Sense. United you stand; divided you fall. I will not be so uncivil as to suggest that Dr. Pym has no common sense; I confine myself to recording the chronological accident that he has not shown us any so far. I take the freedom of an old friend in staking my shirt that Moses has no scientific theory. Yet against this strong coalition I am ready to appear; armed with nothing but an intuition—which is American for a guess."

"Distinguished by Mr. Gould's assistance," said Pym, opening his eyes suddenly. "I gather that though he and I are identical in primary di-agnosis there is yet between us something that cannot be called a disagreement, something which we may perhaps call a—" He put the points of thumb and forefinger together, spreading the other fingers exquisitely in the air, and seemed to be waiting for somebody else to tell him what to say.

"Catchin' flies?" inquired the affable Moses.

"A divergence," said Dr. Pym, with a refined sigh of relief; "a divergence. Granted that the man in question is deranged, he would not necessarily be all that science requires in a homicidal maniac—"

"Has it occurred to you," observed Moon, who was leaning on the gate again, and did not turn round, "that if he were a homicidal maniac he might have killed us all here while we were talking."

Something exploded silently underneath all their minds, like sealed dynamite in some forgotten cellars. They all remembered for the first time for some hour or two that the monster of whom they were talking was standing quite silently among them. They had felt him in the garden like a garden statue; there might have been a dolphin coiling round his legs, or a fountain pouring out of his mouth, for all the notice they had taken of Innocent Smith. He stood with his crest of blonde, blown hair thrust somewhat forward, his fresh-coloured, rather short-sighted face looking patiently downwards at nothing in particular, his huge shoulders humped, and his hands in his trousers' pockets. So far as they could guess he had not moved at all. His green coat might have been cut out of the green turf on which he stood. In his shadow Pym had expounded and Rosamund expostulated; Michael had ranted and Moses had ragged. He had remained like a thing graven; the god of the garden. A sparrow had perched on one of his heavy shoulders; and then, after correcting its costume of feathers, had flown away.

"Why," cried Michael, with a shout of laughter, "the Court of Beacon has opened— and shut up again, too. You all know now I am right. Your buried common sense has told you just what my buried common sense has told me. Smith might have fired off a hundred cannons instead of a pistol, and you would still know he was harmless as I know he is harmless. Back we all go to the house and clear a room for inquiry. For the High Court of Beacon, which has already arrived at its decision, is just about to begin its inquiry."

"Just a goin' to begin!" cried little Mr. Moses in an extraordinary sort of disinterested excitement, like that of an animal during music or a thunderstorm. "Follow on to the 'Igh Court of Eggs and Bacon; 'ave a kipper from the old firm! 'Is Lordship complimented Mr. Gould on the 'igh professional delicacy 'e had shown, and which was worthy of the best traditions of the Saloon Bar—and three of Scotch hot, miss! Oh, chase me, girls!"

The girls betraying no temptation to chase him, he went away in a sort of waddling dance of pure excitement; and had made a circuit of the garden before he reappeared breathless, but still beaming. Moon had known his man when he realized that no people presented to Moses Gould could be quite serious, even if they were quite furious. The glass doors stood open on the side nearest to Mr. Moses Gould; and as the feet of that festive idiot were evidently turned in the same direction, everybody else went that way with the unanimity of some uproarious procession. Only Diana Duke retained enough rigidity to say the thing that had been boiling at her fierce feminine lips for the last few hours. Under the shadow of tragedy she had kept it back as unsympathetic. "In that case," she said sharply, "these cabs can be sent away."

"Well, Innocent must have his bag, you know," said Mary with a smile. "I dare say the cabman would get it down for us."

"I'll get the bag," said Smith, speaking for the first time for hours; his voice sounded remote and rude, like the voice of a statue.

Those who had so long danced and disputed round his immobility were left breathless by his precipitance. With a run and spring he was out of the garden into the street; with a spring and one quivering kick he was actually on the roof of the cab. The cabman happened to be standing by the horse's head, having just removed its emptied nose-bag. Smith seemed for an instant to be rolling about on the cab's back in the embraces of his own Gladstone bag. The next instant, however, he had rolled, as if by a royal luck, into the high seat behind, and with a shriek of piercing and appalling suddenness, had sent the horse flying and scampering far away down the street.

His evanescence was so violent and swift that this time it was all the other people who were turned into garden statues. Mr. Moses Gould, however, being ill-adapted both physically and morally for the purposes of permanent sculpture, came to life sometime before the rest, and, turning to Moon, remarked, like a man starting chattily with a stranger on an omnibus, "Tile loose, eh? Cab loose anyhow." There followed a fatal silence; and then Dr. Warner said, with a sneer like a club of stone,—

"This is what comes of the Court of Beacon, Mr. Moon. You have let loose a maniac on the whole metropolis."

Beacon House stood, as has been said, at the end of a long crescent of continuous houses. The little garden that shut it in ran out into a sharp point like a green cape pushed out into the sea of two streets. Smith and his cab shot up one side of the triangle, and certainly most of those standing inside it never expected to see him again. At the apex, however, he turned the horse sharply round and drove with equal violence up the other side of the garden, visible to all the group. With a common impulse the little crowd ran across the lawn as if to stop him, but they soon had reason to duck and recoil. Even as he vanished up street for the second time, he let the big yellow bag fly from his hand, so that it fell in the centre of the garden, scattering the company like a bomb, and nearly damaging Dr. Warner's hat for the third time. Long before they had collected themselves, the cab had shot away with a shriek that went into a whisper.

"Well," said Michael Moon, with a very queer note in his voice, "you may as well all go inside anyhow. It's getting rather dark and cold. We've got two relics of Mr. Smith at least; his fiancee and his trunk."

"Why do you want us to go inside?" asked Arthur Inglewood, in whose red brow and rough brown hair botheration seemed to have reached its limit.

"I want the rest to go in," said Michael in a clear voice, "because I want the whole of this garden in which to talk to you."

There was an atmosphere of irrational doubt; it was really getting colder, and a night wind had begun to wave the one or two trees in the twilight. Dr. Warner, however, spoke in a voice devoid of indecision.

"I refuse to listen to any such proposal," he said; "you have lost this ruffian, and I must find him."

"I don't ask you to listen to any proposal," answered Moon quietly, "I only ask you to listen."

He made a silencing movement with his hand, and immediately the whistling noise that had been lost in the dark streets on one side of the house could be heard from quite a new quarter on the other side. Through the night-maze of streets the noise increased with incredible rapidity, and the next moment the flying hoofs and flashing wheels had swept up to the blue-railed gate at which they originally stood. Mr. Smith got down from his perch with an air of absent-mindedness, and coming back into the garden stood in the same in an elephantine attitude, as before.

"Get inside! get inside!" cried Moon hilariously, with the air of one shooing a company of cats. "Come, come, be quick about it! Didn't I tell you I wanted to talk to Ingle-wood?"

How they were all really driven into the house again it would have been difficult afterwards to say. They had reached the point of being exhausted with incongruities, as people at a farce are ill with laughing, and the brisk growth of the storm among the trees seemed like a final gesture of things in general. Inglewood lingered behind them, saying with a certain amicable exasperation, "I say, do you really want to speak to me?"

"I do," said Michael, "very much." Night had come as it generally does, quicker than the twilight had seemed to promise. While the human eye still felt the sky as light gray, a very large and lustrous moon appearing abruptly above a bulk of roofs and trees, proved by contrast that the sky was already a very dark gray indeed. A drift of barren leaves across the lawn, a drift of riven clouds across the sky, seemed to be lifted on the same strong and yet laborious wind.

"Arthur," said Michael, "I began with an intuition; but now I am sure. You and I are going to defend this friend of yours before the blessed Court of Beacon, and to clear him, too — clear him both of crime and lunacy. Just listen to me while I preach to you for a bit." They walked up and down the darkening garden together as Michael Moon went on.

"Can you," asked Michael, "shut your eyes and see some of those queer old hieroglyphics they stuck up on white walls in the old hot countries. How stiff they were in shape and yet how gaudy in colour. Think of some alphabet of arbitrary figures picked out in black and red, or white and green, with some old Semitic crowd of Nosey Gould's ancestors staring at it, and try to think why the people put it up at all."

Inglewood's first instinct was to think that his perplexing friend had really gone off his head at last; there seemed so reckless a flight of irrelevancy from the tropic pictured walls he was asked to imagine to the gray, windswept, and somewhat chilly suburban garden in which he was actually kicking his heels. How he could be more happy in one by imagining the other he could not conceive. Both (in themselves) were unpleasant.

"Why does everybody repeat riddles?" went on Moon abruptly; "even if they've forgotten the answers. Riddles are easy to remember because they are hard to guess. So were those stiff old symbols in black, red, or green easy to remember because they had been hard to guess. Their colours were plain. Their shapes were plain. Everything was plain except the meaning."

Inglewood was about to open his mouth in an amiable protest, but Moon went on, plunging quicker and quicker up and down the garden and smoking faster and faster. "Dances, too," he said; "dances were not frivolous. Dances were harder to understand than inscriptions and texts. The old dances were stiff, ceremonial, highly coloured but silent. Have you noticed anything odd about Smith?"

"Well, really," cried Inglewood, left behind in a collapse of humour, "have I noticed anything else about him?"

"Have you noticed this about him," asked Moon, with unshaken persistency, "that he has done so much and said so very little? When first he came he talked, but in a gasping irregular sort of way, as if he wasn't used to it. All he really did was actions—painting red flowers on black gowns or throwing yellow bags on to the grass. I tell you that big green figure is figurative—like any green figure capering on some white Eastern wall."

"My dear Michael," cried Inglewood, in a rising irritation which increased with the rising wind, "you are getting absurdly fanciful."

"I think of what has just happened," said Michael steadily. "The man has not spoken for hours; and yet he has been speaking all the time. He fired three shots from a six-shooter and then gave it up to us, when he might have shot us dead in our boots. How could he express his trust in us better than that? He wanted to be tried by us. How could he have shown it better than by standing quite still and letting us discuss it? He wanted to show that he stood there willingly, and could escape if he liked. How could he have shown it better than by escaping in the cab and coming back again? Innocent Smith is not a madman—he is a ritualist. He wants to express himself, not with his tongue, but with his arms and legs— with my body I thee worship, as it says in the marriage service. I begin to understand the old plays and pageants. I see why the mutes at a funeral were mute. I see why the mummers were mum. They meant something; and Smith means something, too. All other jokes have to be noisy—like little Nosey Gould's jokes, for instance. The only silent jokes are the practical jokes. Poor Smith, properly considered, is an allegorical practical joker. What he has really done in this house has been as frantic as a war-dance, but as silent as a picture."

U I suppose you mean," said the other dubiously, "that we have got to find out what all these crimes meant, as if they were so many coloured picture-puzzles. But even supposing that they do mean something—why, Lord bless my soul!—"

Taking the turn of the garden quite naturally he had lifted his eyes to the moon, by this time risen big and luminous, and had seen a huge, half-human figure sitting on the garden wall. It was outlined so sharply against the moon that for the first flash it was hard to be certain even that it was human: the hunched shoulders and outstanding hair had rather the air of a colossal cat. It resembled a cat also in the fact that when first startled it sprang up and ran with easy activity along the top of the wall. As it ran, however, its heavy shoulders and small stooping head rather suggested a baboon. The instant it came within reach of a tree it made an ape-like leap and was lost in the

134

MANALIVE

branches. The gale, which by this time was shaking every shrub in the garden, made the identification yet more difficult, since it melted the moving limbs of the fugitive in the multitudinous moving limbs of the tree.

"Who is there?" shouted Arthur. "Who are you? Are you Innocent?"

"Not quite," answered an obscure voice among the leaves. "I cheated you once about a penknife."

The wind in the garden had gathered strength, and was throwing the tree backwards and forwards with the man in the thick of it, just as it had on the gay and golden afternoon when he had first arrived.

"But are you Smith?" asked Inglewood, as in an agony.

"Very nearly," said the voice out of the tossing tree.

"But you must have some real names," shrieked Inglewood in despair. "You must call yourself something."

"Call myself something," thundered the obscure, shaking the tree so that all its ten hundred leaves seemed to be talking at once. "I call myself Roland Oliver Isiah Charlemagne

MANALIVE

Arthur Hildebrand Homer Danton Michael Angelo Shakespeare Brakespeare—"

"But, manalive!" began Inglewood in exasperation.

"That's right! that's right!" came with a roar out of the rocking tree; "that's my real name." And he broke a branch, and one or two autumn leaves fluttered away across the moon.

PART II

THE EXPLANATIONS OF INNOCENT SMITH

CHAPTER I

THE EYE OF DEATH; OR, THE MURDER CHARGE

THE dining-room of the Dukes had been set out for the Court of Beacon with a certain impromptu pomposity, that seemed somehow to increase its cosiness. The big room was, as it were, cut up into small rooms, with walls only waist high, the sort of separations that children make when they are playing at shops. This had been done by Moses Gould and Michael Moon (the two most active members of this remarkable inquiry) with the ordinary furniture of the place. At one end of the long mahogany table was set the one enormous garden chair, which was sur-

MAN ALIVE

mounted by the old torn tent or umbrella which Smith himself had suggested as a coronation canopy. Inside this erection could be perceived the dumpy form of Mrs. Duke, with cushions and a form of countenance that already threatened slumber. At the other end sat the accused Smith, in a kind of dock; for he was carefully fenced in with a quadrilateral of light bedroom chairs, any of which he could have tossed out of the window with his big toe. He had been provided with pens and paper, out of the latter of which he made paper boats, paper darts, and paper dolls contentedly through the whole proceedings. He never spoke or even looked up, but seemed as unconscious as a child on the floor of an empty nursery.

On a row of chairs, raised high on the top of a long settee, sat the three young ladies with their backs up against the window, and Mary Gray in the middle; it was something between a jury box and the stall of the Queen of Beauty at a tournament. Down the centre of the long table,

Moon had built a low barrier out of eight bound volumes of "Good Words" to express the moral wall that divided the conflicting parties. On the right side sat the two advocates of the prosecution, Dr. Pym and Mr. Gould, behind a barricade of books and documents, chiefly (in the case of Dr. Pym) solid volumes of criminology. On the other side, Moon and Inglewood, for the defence, were also fortified with books and papers, but as these included several old yellow volumes by Ouida and Wilkie Collins, the hand of Mr. Moon seemed to have been somewhat careless and comprehensive. As for the victim and prosecutor, Dr. Warner, Moon wanted at first to have him kept entirely behind a high screen in the corner, urging the indelicacy of his appearance in court, but privately assuring him of an unofficial permission to peep over the top now and then. Dr. Warner, however, failed to rise to the chivalry of such a course, and after some little disturbance and discussion, he was accommodated with a seat on the right side of the table in a line with his legal advisers.

It was before this solidly established tribunal that Dr. Cyrus Pym, after passing a hand through the honey-coloured hair over each ear, rose to open the case. His statement was clear and even restrained, and such flights of imagery as occurred in it only attracted attention by a certain indescribable abruptness, not uncommon in the flowers of American speech.

He planted the points of his ten frail fingers on the mahogany, closed his eyes, and opened his mouth. "The time has gone by," he said, "when murder could be regarded as a moral and individual act, important perhaps to the murderer, perhaps to the murdered. Science has profoundly . . ." Here he paused, poising his compressed finger and thumb in the air as if he were holding an elusive idea very tight by its tail, then he screwed up his eyes and said: "modified," and let it go; "has profoundly modified one view of death. In superstitious ages it was regarded as the termination of life, catastrophic, and even tragic, and was often surrounded with solemnity. Brighter days, however, have dawned, and we now see death as universal and inevitable, as part of that great soul stirring and heart upholding average, which we call for convenience, the order of nature. In the same way we have come to considerable murder socially. Rising above the mere private feelings of a man while being forcibly deprived of life, we are privileged to behold murder as a mighty whole, to see the rich rotation of the cosmos, bringing, as it brings the golden harvests and the golden-bearded harvesters, the return for ever of the slayers and the slain."

He looked down, somewhat affected with his own eloquence, coughed slightly, putting up four of his pointed fingers with the excellent manners of Boston, and continued, "There is but one result of this happier and humaner outlook which concerns the wretched man before us. It is that thoroughly elucidated by a Milwaukee doctor, our great secret-guessing Sonneuschein, in his great work, 'The Destructive Type.' We do not denounce Smith as a murderer, but rather as a murderous man. The type is such that its very life—I might say its very health—is in killing. Some hold that it is not properly an aberration, but a newer and even a higher creature. My dear old friend Dr. Bulger, who kept ferrets—" (here Moon suddenly ejaculated a loud "hurrah!" but so instantaneously resumed his tragic expression that Mrs. Duke looked everywhere else for the origin of the sound) ; Dr. Pym continued somewhat sternly—"who, in the interests of knowledge, kept ferrets, held that the creatures' ferocity is not utilitarian, but absolutely an end in itself. However this may be with ferrets, it is certainly so with the prisoner. In his other iniquities you may find the cunning of the maniac; but his acts of blood have almost the simplicity of sanity. But it is the awful sanity of the sun and the elements—a cruel, an evil sanity. As soon stay the iris-leapt cataracts of our virgin West as stay the natural force that sends him forth to slay. No environment, however scientific, could have softened him. Place that man in the silver-silent purity of the palest cloister, and there will be some deed of violence done with the crozier or the alb. Rear him in a happy nursery, amid the brave-browed Anglo-Saxon infancy, and he will find some way to strangle with the skipping-rope or to brain with the brick. Circumstances may be favourable, training may be admirable, hopes may be high, but the huge elemental hunger of Innocent Smith for blood will in its appointed season burst like a well-timed bomb."

Arthur Inglewood glanced curiously for an instant at the huge creature at the foot of the table, who was fitting a paper figure with a paper cocked hat, and then looked back at Dr. Pym, who was concluding in a quieter tone.

"It only remains for us," he said, "to bring forward actual evidence of his previous attempts. By an agreement already made with the Court and the leaders of the defence, we are permitted to put in evidence authentic letters from witnesses to these scenes, which the defence is free to examine. Out of several cases of such outrages we have decided to select one—the clearest and most scandalous. I will therefore, without further delay, call on my junior, Mr. Gould, to read two letters—one from the Sub-Warden and the other from the porter of Brakespeare College, in Cambridge University."

Gould jumped up with a jerk like a jack-in-the-box, an academic-looking paper in his hand and a fever of importance on his face. He began in a loud, high cockney voice that was as abrupt as cock-crow,—

" 'SIR,—Hi am the Sub-Warden of Brike-speare College, Cimbridge—' "

"Lord have mercy on us," muttered Moon, making a backward movement as men do when a gun goes off.

" 'Hi am the Sub-Warden of Brikespeare College, Cimbridge,' " proclaimed the uncompromising Moses, " 'and I can endorse the description you give of the conduct of the un-'appy Smith. It was not alone my unfortunate duty to rebuke many of the lesser violences of his undergraduate period, but I was actually a witness to the last iniquity which terminated that period. Hi happened to be passing under the house of my friend the Warden of Brikespeare, which is semi-detached from the College and connected with it by two or three very ancient arches or props, like bridges across a small strip of water connected with the river. To my grive astonishment I be'eld my eminent friend suspended in mid-air and clinging to one of these pieces of masonry, his appearance and attitude in-dicatin' that he suffered from the grivest ap-

prehensions. After a short time I heard two very loud shots, and distinctly perceived the unfortunate undergraduate Smith leaning far out of the Warden's window and aiming at the Warden repeatedly with a revolver. Upon seeing me, Smith burst into a loud laugh (in which impertinence was mingled with insanity), and appeared to desist. I sent the college porter for a ladder, and he succeeded in detaching the Warden from his painful position. Smith was sent down. The photograph I enclose is from the group of the University Rifle Club Prizemen, and represents him as he was when at the College.—Hi am, your obedient servant, AMOS BOULTER.'

"The other letter," continued Gould in a glow of triumph, "is from the porter, and won't take long to read,—

u 'Dear Sir, —It is quite true that I am the porter of Brikespeare College, and that I 'elped the Warden down when the young man was shooting at him, as Mr. Boulter has said in his letter. The young man who was shooting was Mr. Smith, the same that is in the photo-

graph Mr. Boulter sends.—Yours respect-fully,

" 'Samuel Barker.* "

Gould handed the two letters across to Moon, who examined them. But for the vocal divergences in the matter of h's and a's, the Sub-Warden's letter was exactly as Gould had rendered it; and both that and the porter's letter were plainly genuine. Moon handed them to Inglewood, who handed them back in silence to Moses Gould.

"So far as this first charge of continual attempted murder is concerned," said Dr. Pym, standing up for the last time, "that is my case."

Michael Moon rose for the defence with an air of depression which gave little hope at the outset to the sympathizers with the prisoner. He did not, he said, propose to follow the doctor into the abstract questions. "I do not know enough to be an agnostic," he said rather wearily, "and I can only master the known and admitted elements in such controversies. As for science and religion, the known and admitted facts are few and plain enough. All that the parsons say is unproved. All that the doctors say is disproved. That's the only difference between science and religion there's ever been, or will be. Yet these new discoveries touch me, somehow," he said, looking down sorrowfully at his boots. "They remind me of a dear old great-aunt of mine who used to enjoy them in her youth. It brings tears to my eyes. I can see the old bucket by the garden fence and the line of shimmering poplars behind—"

"Hi! here, stop the bus a bit," cried Mr. Moses Gould, rising in a sort of perspiration; "we want to give the defence a fair run—like gents, you know. But any gent would draw the line at shimmering poplars."

"Well, hang it all," said Moon, in an injured manner, "If Dr. Pym may have an old friend with ferrets, why mayn't I have an old aunt with poplars?"

"I am sure," said Mrs. Duke, bridling, with something almost like a shaky authority, "Mr. Moon may have what aunts he likes."

"Why as to liking her," began Moon, "I— but perhaps as you say she is scarcely the core of the question. I repeat that I do not mean to follow the abstract speculations. For indeed my answer to Dr. Pym is simple and severely concrete. Dr. Pym has only treated one side of the psychology of murder. If it be true that there is a kind of man who has a natural tendency to murder, is it not equally true—" here he lowered his voice and spoke with a crushing quietude and earnestness, "is it not equally true that there is a kind of man who has a natural tendency to get murdered? Is it not at least a hypothesis holding the field that Dr. Warner is such a man? I do not speak without the book, any more than my learned friend. The whole matter is expounded in Dr. Mooneushein's monumental work, 'The Destructible Doctor,' with diagrams showing the various ways in which such a person as Dr. Warner may be resolved into his elements. In the light of these facts—'"

"Hi, stop the bus! stop the bus!" cried Moses, jumping up and gesticulating in great excitement. "My principal's got something to say! My principal wants to do a bit of talkin'."

Dr. Pym was indeed on his feet looking pallid and rather vicious. "I have strictly con-fined myself," he said nasally, "to books to which immediate reference can be made. I have Sonneuschein's 'Destructive Type' here on the table, if the defence wish to see it. Where is this wonderful work on Destructi-bility Mr. Moon is talking about? Does it exist? Can he produce it?"

"Produce it!" cried the Irishman with a rich scorn. "I'll produce it in a week if you'll pay for the ink and paper."

"Would it have much authority?" asked Pym, sitting down.

"Oh, authority!" said Moon lightly, "that depends on a fellow's religion."

Dr. Pym jumped up again. "Our authority is based on masses of accurate detail," he said. "It deals with a region in which things can be handled and tested. My opponent will at least admit that death is a fact of experience."

"Not of mine," said Moon mournfully, shaking his head. "I've never experienced such a thing in my life."

"Well, really," said Dr. Pym, and sat down sharply amid a crackle of papers.

"So we see," resumed Moon, in the same melancholy voice, "that a man like Dr. Warner is, in the mysterious workings of evolution, doomed to such attacks. My Client's onslaught, even if it occurred, was not unique. I have in my hand letters from more than one acquaintance of Dr. Warner whom that remarkable man has affected in the same way. Following the example of my learned friends I will read only two of them. The first is from an honest and laborious matron living off the Harrow Road,—

" 'Mr. Moon, Sir,— Yes, I did throw a sorsepan at him. Wot then? It was all I had to throw, all the soft things being porned, an' if your Doctor Warner doesn't like having sorsepans thrown at him don't let him were his hat in a respectible woman's parler, and tell him to leave orf smiling or tell us the joke.— Yours respectfully, HANNAH MILES.'

"The other letter is from a physician of some note in Dublin, with whom Dr. Warner was once engaged in consultation. He writes as follows,—

" 'Dear Sir, —The incident to which you refer is one which I regret, and which, more-over, I have never been able to explain. My own branch of medicine is not mental; and I should be glad to have the view of a mental specialist on my singular momentary and indeed almost automatic action. To say that I "pulled Dr. Warner's nose" is, however, inaccurate in a respect that strikes me as important. That I punched his nose I must cheerfully admit (I need not say with what regret), but pulling seems to me to imply a precision of handling and an exactitude of objective with which I cannot reproach myself; in comparison with this, the act of punching was an outward, instantaneous and even natural gesture. —Believe me, yours faithfully,

" 'Burton Lestrange.'

"I have numberless other letters," continued Moon, "all bearing witness to this widespread feeling about my eminent friend; and I therefore think that Dr. Pym should have admitted this side of the question into his survey. We are in the presence, as Dr. Pym so truly says, of a natural force. As soon stay the cataracts of the London water-works as stay the great tendency of Dr. Warner to be assassinated by

somebody. Place that man in a Quakers meeting, among the most peaceful of Christians, and he will immediately be beaten to death with sticks of chocolate. Place him among the angels of the New Jerusalem, and he will be stoned to death with precious stones. Circumstances may be beautiful and wonderful, the average may be heart-upholding, the harvester may be golden-bearded, the doctor may be secret-guessing, the cataract may be iris-leapt, the Anglo-Saxon infant may be brave-browed, but against and above all these prodigies the grand simple tendency of Dr. Warner to get murdered will still pursue its way until it happily and triumphantly succeeds at last."

He pronounced this peroration with an appearance of strong emotion; but even stronger emotions were manifesting themselves on the other side of the table. Dr. Warner had leaned his large body quite across the little figure of Moses Gould and was talking in excited whispers to Dr. Pym. That expert nodded a great many times and finally started to his feet with a sincere expression of sternness.

"Ladies and gentlemen," he cried indig-

nantly, "as my colleague has said, we should be delighted to give any latitude to the defence —if there were a defence. But Mr. Moon seems to think he is there to make jokes—very good jokes I dare say, but not at all adapted to assist his client. He picks holes in science. He picks holes in my client's social popularity. He picks holes in my literary style, which doesn't seem to suit his high-toned European taste. But how does this picking of holes effect the issue? This Smith has picked two holes in my client's hat; and with an inch better aim would have picked two holes in his head. All the jokes in the world won't unpick those holes or be any use for the defence."

Inglewood looked down in some embarrassment as if shaken by the evident fairness of this, but Moon still gazed at his opponent in a dreamy way. "The defence?" he said vaguely; "oh, I haven't begun that yet."

"You certainly have not," said Pym warmly, amid a murmur of applause from his side, which the other side found it impossible to answer. "Perhaps, if you have any defence, which has been doubtful from the very beginning—"

"While you're standing up," said Moon, in the same almost sleepy style, "perhaps I might ask you a question."

"A question? Certainly," said Pym stiffly. "It was distinctly arranged between us that as we could not cross-examine the witnesses, we might vicariously cross-examine each other. We are in a position to invite all such inquiry."

"I think you said," observed Moon absently, "that none of the prisoner's shots really hit the doctor."

"For the cause of science," cried the complacent Pym, "fortunately not."

"Yet they were fired from a few feet away."

"Yes; about four feet."

"And no shots hit the Warden, though they were fired quite close to him, too?" asked

Moon.

"That is so," said the witness gravely.

"I think," said Moon, suppressing a slight yawn, "that your Sub-Warden mentioned that Smith was one of the university record men for shooting."

"Why, as to that—" began Pym, after an instant of stillness.

"A second question," continued Moon comparatively curtly. "You said there were other cases of the accused trying to kill other people. Why have you not got evidence of them?"

The American planted the points of his fingers on the table again. "In those cases," he said precisely, "there was no evidence from outsiders, as in the Cambridge case, but only the evidence of the actual victims."

"Why didn't you get their evidence?"

"In the case of the actual victims," said Pym, "there was some difficulty and reluctance, and—"

"Do you mean," asked Moon, "that none of the actual victims would appear against the prisoner?"

"That would be exaggerative," began the other.

"A third question," said Moon, so sharply that every one jumped. "YouVe got the evidence of the Sub-Warden who heard some shots. Where's the evidence of the Warden himself who was shot at? The Warden of Brakespeare lives, a prosperous gentleman."

"We did ask for a statement from him," said Pym a little nervously; "but it was so eccentrically expressed that we suppressed it out of deference to an old gentleman whose past services to science have been great."

Moon leaned forward. "You mean, I suppose," he said, "that his statement was favourable to the prisoner."

"It might be understood so," replied the American doctor; "but really it was difficult to understand at all. In fact, we sent it back to him."

"You have no longer, then, any statement signed by the Warden of Brakespeare."

"No."

"I only ask," said Michael quietly, "because we have. To conclude my case I will ask my junior, Mr. Inglewood, to read a statement of the true story, a statement attested as true by the signature of the Warden himself."

Arthur Inglewood rose with several papers in his hand, and though he looked somewhat refined and self-effacing, as he always did, the spectators were surprised to feel that his presence was upon the whole more efficient and sufficing than his leader's. He was, in truth, one of those modest men who cannot speak until they are told to speak; and then can speak well. Moon was entirely the opposite. His own impudences amused him in private, but they slightly embarrassed him in public; he felt a fool while he was speaking, whereas Inglewood felt a fool only because he could not speak. The moment he had anything to say he could speak; and the moment he could speak, speaking seemed quite natural. Nothing in this universe seemed quite natural to Michael Moon.

"As my colleague has just explained," said Inglewood, "there are two enigmas or inconsistencies on which we base the defence. The first is a plain physical fact. By the admission of everybody, by the very evidence adduced by the prosecution, it is clear that the accused was celebrated as a specially good shot. Yet on both the occasions complained of, he shot at a man from about four or five feet and shot at him four or five times, and never hit him once. That is the first startling circumstance on which we base our argument. The second, as my colleague has urged, is the curious fact that we cannot find a single victim of these alleged outrages to speak for himself. Subordinates speak for him. Porters

climb up ladders to him. But he himself is silent. Ladies and gentlemen, I propose to explain on the spot both the riddle of the shots and the riddle of the silence. I will first of all read the covering letter in which the true account of the Cambridge incident is contained, and then that document itself. When you have heard both, there will be no doubt about your decision. The covering letter runs as follows,—

" 'Dear Sir, —The following is a very exact and even vivid account of the incident as it really happened at Brakespeare College. We, the undersigned, do not see any particular reason why we should refer it to any isolated authorship. The truth is, it has been a composite production; and we have even had some difference of opinion about the adjectives. But every word of it is true,—We are, yours faithfully,

" Wilfred Emerson Eames,
" 'Warden of Brakespeare College, Cambridge.
" 'Innocent Smith.'

"The enclosed statement," continued Ingle-wood, "runs as follows,—

" 'A celebrated English university backs so abruptly on the river that it has, so to speak, to be propped up and patched with all sorts of bridges and semi-detached buildings. The river itself splits into several small streams and canals, so that in one or two corners the place has almost the look of Venice. It was so, specially in the case with which we are concerned, in which a few flying buttresses or airy ribs of stone sprang across a strip of water to connect Brakespeare College with the house of the Warden of Brakespeare.

" 'The country around these colleges is flat; but it does not seem flat when one is thus in the midst of the colleges. For in these flat fens there are always wandering lakes and lingering rivers of water. And these always change what might have been a scheme of horizontal lines into a scheme of vertical lines. Wherever there is water, the height of high buildings is doubled, and a British brick house becomes a Babylonian tower. In that shining

unshaken surface the houses hang head downwards exactly to their highest or lowest chimney. The coral-coloured cloud seen in that abyss is as far below the world as its original appears above it. Every scrap of water is not only a window but a skylight. Earth breaks under men's feet into precipitous aerial perspectives, into which a bird could as easily wing its way as—' "

Dr. Cyrus Pym rose in protest. The documents he had put in evidence had been confined to cold affirmations of fact. The defence, in a general way, had an indubitable right to put their case in their own way. But all this landscape gardening seemed to him (Dr. Cyrus Pym) to be not up to the business. "Will the leader of the defence tell me," he asked, "how it can possibly affect this case, that a cloud was cor'l-coloured, or that the river was unshaken and shiny, or that a bird could have winged itself anywhere?"

"Oh, I don't know," said Michael, lifting himself lazily; "you see, you don't know yet what our defence is. Till you know that, don't you see, anything may be relevant.

Why, suppose," he said suddenly, as if an idea had struck him, "suppose we wanted to prove the old Warden colour-blind. Suppose he was shot by a black man with white hair, when he thought he was being shot by a white man with yellow hair. To ascertain if that cloud was really and truly coral-coloured might be of the most massive importance."

He paused with a seriousness which was hardly commonly shared, and continued with the same fluency. "Or suppose we wanted to maintain that the Warden committed suicide. That he just got Smith to hold the pistol as Brutus's slave held the sword. Why, it would make all the difference whether the Warden could see himself plain in still water. Still water has made hundreds of suicides. One sees oneself so very—well, so very plain."

"Do you, perhaps," inquired Pym with austere irony, "maintain that your client was a bird of some sort—say, a flamingo?"

"In the matter of his being a flamingo," said Moon with sudden severity, "my client reserves his defence."

No one quite knowing what to make of this, Mr. Moon resumed his seat with an air of great sternness, and Inglewood resumed the reading of his document.

"There is something pleasing to a mystic in such a land of mirrors. For a mystic is one who holds that two worlds are better than one. In the highest sense indeed, all thought is reflection.

"This is the real truth in the saying that second thoughts are best. Animals have no second thoughts; man alone is able to see his own thought double, as a drunkard sees a lamp-post. Man alone is able to see his own thought upside down as one sees a house in a puddle. This duplication of mentality, as in a mirror, is (we repeat) the inmost thing of human philosophy. There is a mystical, even a monstrous truth in the statement that two heads are better than one. But they ought both to grow on the same body.'

"I know it's a little transcendental at first," interposed Inglewood, beaming round with a broad apology, "but you see this document was written in collaboration by a don and a—"

"Drunkard, eh?" suggested Moses Gould, beginning to enjoy himself.

"I rather think," proceeded Inglewood, with an unruffled and critical air, "that this part was written by the don. I merely warn the court that the statement, though indubitably accurate, bears here and there the trace of coming from two authors."

"In that case," said Dr. Pym, leaning back and sniffing, "I cannot agree with them that two heads are better than one."

"The undersigned persons think it needless to touch on a kindred problem so often discussed at committees for university reform; the question of whether dons see double because they are drunk or get drunk because they see double. It is enough for them (the undersigned persons) if they are able to pursue their own peculiar and profitable theme—which is puddles. What (the undersigned persons ask themselves) is a puddle? A puddle repeats infinity, and is full of light; nevertheless, if analyzed objectively, a puddle is a piece of dirty water spread very thin on mud. The two great historic universities of England have all this large and level and reflective brilliance. They repeat infinity. They are full of light. Nevertheless, or rather on the other hand, they are puddles. Puddles, puddles, puddles, puddles. The undersigned persons ask you to excuse an emphasis inseparable from strong conviction.' "

Inglewood ignored a somewhat wild expression on the faces of some present, and continued with eminent cheerfulness.

" 'Such were the thoughts that failed to cross the mind of the undergraduate Smith as he picked his way among the stripes of canal and the glittering rainy gutters, into which the water broke up round the back of Brakespeare College. Had these thoughts crossed his mind he would have been very much happier than he was. Unfortunately he did not know that his puzzles were puddles. He did not know that the academic mind reflects infinity, and is full of light by the simple process of being shallow and standing still. In his case, therefore, there was something solemn, and even evil about the infinity implied. It was half-way through a starry night of bewildering brilliancy, stars were both above and below. To young Smith's sullen fancy, the skies below seemed even hollower than the skies above. He had a horrible idea that if he counted the stars he would find one too many in the pool.

" 'In crossing the little paths and bridges he felt like one stepping on the black and slender ribs of some cosmic Eiffel Tower. For to him, and nearly all the educated youth of that epoch, the stars were cruel things; though they glowed in the great dome every night, they were an enormous and ugly secret; they uncovered the nakedness of nature; they were a glimpse of the iron wheels and pulleys behind the scenes. For the young men of that sad time thought that the god always came from the machine. They did not know that in reality the machine only comes from the god. In short, they were all pessimists, and starlight was atrocious to them—atrocious because it was true. All their universe was black with white spots.

" 'Smith looked up with relief from the glittering pools below to the glittering skies and the great black bulk of the college. The only light other than stars glowed through one peacock-green curtain in the upper part of the building, marking where Dr. Emerson Eames always worked till morning and received his friends and favourite pupils at any hour of the night. Indeed, it was to his rooms that the melancholy Smith was bound. Smith had been at Dr. Eames's lecture for the first half of the morning, and at pistol practice and fencing in a saloon for the second half. He had been sculling madly for the first half of the afternoon and thinking idly (and still more madly) for the second half. He had gone to a supper where he was uproarious, and on to a debating club where he was perfectly insufferable, and the melancholy Smith was melancholy still. Then, as he was going home to his diggings, he remembered the eccentricity of his friend and master, the Warden of Brakespeare, and resolved desperately to turn in to that gentleman's private house.

11 'Emerson Eames was an eccentric in many ways, but his throne in philosophy and metaphysics was of international eminence; the university could hardly have afforded to lose him, and, moreover, a don has only to continue any of his bad habits long enough to make them a part of the British constitution. The bad

habits of Emerson Eames were to sit up all night and to be a student of Schopenhauer. Personally, he was a lean, lounging sort of man, with a blond pointed beard, not so very much older than his pupil Smith in the matter of mere years, but older by centuries in the two essential respects of having a European reputation and a bald head.

"I came to see you at this unearthly hour," said Smith, who was nothing to the eye except a very big man trying to make himself small, "because I am coming to the conclusion that existence is really too rotten. I know all the arguments of the thinkers that think otherwise, bishops and agnostics and those sort of people. And knowing you were the greatest living authority on the pessimist thinkers—"

"All thinkers," said Eames, "are pessimist thinkers."

After a patch of pause, not the first—for this depressing conversation had gone on for some hours with alternations of cynicism and silence—the Warden continued with his air of weary brilliancy. "It's all a question of wrong calculation. The moth flies into the candle because he doesn't happen to know that the game is not worth the candle. The wasp gets into the jam in hearty and hopeful efforts to get the jam into him. In the same way the vulgar people want to enjoy life just as they want to enjoy gin—because they are too stupid to see that they are paying too big a price for it. That they never find happiness, that they don't even know how to look for it, is proved by the paralyzing clumsiness and ugliness of everything they do. Their discordant colours are cries of pain. Look at the brick villas beyond the college on this side of the river. There's one with spotted blinds; look at it! just go and look at it!"

"Of course," he went on dreamily, "one or two men see the sober fact a long way off, they go mad. Do you notice that maniacs mostly try either to destroy other things, or (if they are thoughtful) to destroy themselves. The madman is the man behind the scenes, like the man that wanders about the coulisse of a theatre. He has only opened the wrong door, and come into the right place. He sees things at the right angle. But the common world—"

"Oh, hang the world!" said the sullen Smith, letting his fist fall on the table in an idle despair.

"Let's give it a bad name first," said the Professor calmly, "and then hang it. A puppy with hydrophobia would probably struggle for life while we killed it; but if we were kind we should kill it. So an omniscient god would put us out of our pain. He would strike us dead."

"Why doesn't he strike us dead?" asked the undergraduate abstractedly, plunging his hands into his pockets.

"He is dead himself," said the philosopher; "that is where he is really enviable."

"To any one who thinks," proceeded Eames, "the pleasures of life trivial and soon tasteless, are bribes to bring us into a torture chamber. We all see that for any thinking man mere extinction is the . . . What are you doing? . . . Are you mad? . . . Put that thing down."

Dr. Eames had turned his tired but still talkative head over his shoulder, and had found himself looking into a small, round, black hole, rimmed by a six-sided circlet of steel, with a sort of spike standing up on the top. It fixed him like an iron eye. Through those eternal instants during which the reason is stunned, he did not even know what it was. Then he saw behind it the chambered barrel and cocked hammer of a revolver, and behind that the flushed and rather heavy face of Smith, apparently quite unchanged, or even more mild than before.

"I'll help you out of your hole, old man," said Smith, with rough tenderness. "I'll put the puppy out of his pain."

Emerson Eames retreated towards the window. "Do you mean to kill me?" he cried.

"It's not a thing I'd do for every one," said Smith, with emotion. "But you and I seem to have got so intimate to-night, somehow. I know all your troubles now, and the only cure, old chap."

"Put that thing down," shouted the Warden.

"It'll soon be over, you know," said Smith, with the air of a sympathetic dentist.

And as the Warden made a run for the window and balcony, his benefactor followed him with a quick step and a compassionate expression.

Both men were perhaps surprised to see that the gray and white of early daybreak had already come. One of them, however, had emotions calculated to swallow up surprise. Brakespeare College was one of the few that retained real traces of Gothic ornament, and just beneath Dr. Eames's balcony there ran out what had once been a flying buttress, still shapelessly shaped into gray beasts and devils, but blinded with mosses and washed out with rains. With an ungainly and most courageous leap, Eames sprang out on this antique bridge, as the only possible mode of escape from the maniac. He sat astride of it, still in his academic gown, dangling his long thin legs, and considering further chances of flight. The whitening daylight opened under as well as over him that impression of vertical infinity we have remarked about the little lakes round Brakespeare. Looking down and seeing the spires and chimneys pendent in the pools, they felt alone in space. They felt as if they were peering over the edge from the North Pole and seeing the South Pole below.

"Hang the world, we said," observed Smith, "and the world is hanged. He has hanged the world upon nothing, says the Bible. Do you like being hanged upon nothing? I'm going to be hanged on something myself. I'm going to swing for you . . . Dear, tender old phrase," he murmured; "never true till this moment. I am going to swing for you. For you, dear friend. For your sake. At your express desire."

"Help!" cried the Warden of Brakes-peare College; "help!"

"The puppy struggles," said the undergraduate, with an eye of pity; "the poor little puppy struggles. How fortunate it is that I am wiser and kinder than he," and he sighted his weapon so as exactly to cover the upper part of Eames's bald head.

"Smith," said the philosopher, with a sudden change to a sort of ghastly lucidity, "I shall go mad."

"And so look at things from the right angle," observed Smith, sighing gently. "Ah, but madness is only a palliative at best, a drug. The only cure is an operation—an operation that is always successful: death."

As he spoke the sun rose. It seemed to put colour into everything, with the rapidity of a lightning artist. A fleet of little clouds sailing across the sky changed from pigeon-gray to pink. All over the little academic town the tops of different buildings took on different tints; here the sun would pick out the green enamel on a pinnacle, there the scarlet tiles of a villa; here the copper ornament on some artistic shop, and there the sea-blue slates of some old and steep church roof. All these coloured crests seemed to have something oddly individual and significant about them, like crests of famous knights pointed out in a pageant or a battlefield; they each arrested the eye, especially the rolling eye of Emerson Eames as he looked round on the morning and accepted it as his last. Through a narrow chink between a black timber tavern and a big gray college he could see a clock with gilt hands, which the sunshine set on fire. He stared at it as though hypnotized; and suddenly the clock began to strike, as if in personal reply. As if at a signal, clock after

clock took up the cry. All the churches awoke like chickens at cockcrow. The birds were already noisy in the trees behind the college. The sun rose, gathering glory that seemed too full for the deep skies to hold, and the shallow waters beneath them seemed golden and brimming and deep enough for the thirst of the gods. Just round the corner of the college, and visible from his crazy perch, were the brightest specks on that bright landscape, the villas with the spotted blinds, which he had made his text that night. He wondered for the first time what people lived in them.

" 'Suddenly he called out with mere querulous authority, as he might have called to a student to shut a door.

" * "Let me come off this place," he cried; "I can't bear it."

" ' "I rather doubt if it will bear you," said Smith critically; "but before you break your neck, or I blow out your brains, or let you back into this room (on which complex points I am undecided), I want the metaphysical point cleared up. Do I understand that you want to get back to life?"

" * "I'd give anything to get back," replied the unhappy professor.

""Give anything!" cried Smith; "then blast your impudence, give us a song!"

" ' "What do you mean?" demanded the exasperated Eames; "what song?"

" ' "A hymn, I think, would be most appropriate," answered the other gravely. "I'll let you off if you'll repeat after me the words—

" 'I thank the goodness and the grace That on my birth have smiled, And perched me on this curious place, A happy English child.' "

" 'Dr. Emerson Eames having briefly complied, his persecutor abruptly told him to hold his hands up in the air. Vaguely connecting this proceeding with the usual conduct of brigands and bushrangers, Mr. Eames held them up, very stiffly, but without marked surprise. A bird alighted on his stone seat, took no more notice of him than of a comic statue.

" ' "You are now engaged in public worship," remarked Smith severely, "and before I have done with you, you shall thank God for the very ducks on the pond."

" 'The celebrated pessimist half-articulately expressed his perfect readiness to thank God for the ducks on the pond.

""Not forgetting the drakes," said Smith sternly. (Eames weakly conceded the drakes.) "Not forgetting anything, please. You shall thank heaven for churches and chapels and villas and vulgar people and puddles and pots and pans and sticks and rags and bones and spotted blinds."

" ' "All right, all right," repeated the victim in despair; "sticks and rags and bones and blinds."

" ' "Spotted blinds, I think we said," remarked Smith with a roguish ruthlessness, and wagging the pistol-barrel at him like a long metallic ringer.

" ' "Spotted blinds," said Emerson Eames, faintly.

"You can't say fairer than that," admitted the younger man, "and now I'll just tell you this to wind up with. If you really were what you profess to be, I don't see that it would matter to snail or seraph if you broke your impious stiff neck, and dashed out all your drivelling devil-worshipping brains. But, in strict biographical fact, you are a very nice fellow, addicted to talking putrid nonsense, and I love you like a brother. I shall, therefore, fire off all my cartridges round your head so as not to hit you (I am a good shot, you may be glad to hear), and then we will go in and have some breakfast."

"He let off two barrels in the air, which the Professor endured with singular firmness, and then said, "But don't fire them all off."

"Why not?" asked the other buoyantly.

"Keep them," answered his companion, "for the next man you meet who talks as we were talking."

"It was at this moment that Smith, looking down, perceived apopletic terror upon the face of the Sub-Warden, and heard the donnish shriek with which he summoned the porter and the ladder.

"It took Dr. Eames some little time to disentangle himself from the ladder, and some little time longer to disentangle himself from the Sub-Warden. But as soon as he could do so unobtrusively, he rejoined his companion in the late extraordinary scene. He was astonished to find the gigantic Smith heavily shaken, and sitting with his shaggy head on his hands. When addressed, he lifted a very pale face.

"Why, what is the matter?" asked Eames, whose own nerves had by this time twittered themselves quiet, like the morning birds.

"I must ask your indulgence," said Smith, rather brokenly. "I must ask you to realize that I have just had an escape from death."

"You have had an escape from death?" repeated the Professor in not unpardonable irritation; "well, of all the cheek—"

"Oh, don't you understand, don't you understand?" cried the pale young man impatiently; "I had to do it, Eames. I had to prove you wrong or die. When a man's young he nearly always has some one whom he thinks the top water mark of the mind of man—some one who knows all about it, if anybody knows.

"Wd^ you were that to me; you spoke with authority, and not as the scribes. Nobody could comfort me if you said there was no comfort. If you really thought there was nothing anywhere, it was because you had been there to see. Don't you see that I had to prove you didn't really mean it? Or else drown myself in the canal."

"Well," said Eames hesitatingly, "I think perhaps you confuse—"

"Oh, don't tell me that," cried Smith, with the sudden clairvoyance of mental pain; "don't tell me that I confuse enjoyment of existence with the Will to Live. That's German, and German is High Dutch, and High Dutch is Double Dutch. The thing I saw shining in your eyes when you dangled on that bridge was enjoyment of life and not 'the Will to Live.' What you knew when you sat on that damned gargoyle was, that the world, when all is said and done, is a wonderful and beautiful place; I know it, because I knew it at the same minute. I saw the gray clouds turn pink, and the little gilt clock in the crack between the houses. It was those things you hated leaving, not Life, whatever that is. Eames, we've been to the brink of death together; won't you admit I am right?"

" * "Yes," said Eames very slowly, "I think you are right. You shall have an alpha-plus."

"'Right!" cried Smith, springing up reanimated. "I've passed with honours, and now let me go and see about being sent down."

u i «y ou needn't be sent down," said Eames, with the quiet confidence of twelve years of intrigue; "everything with us comes from the man on top to the people just round him. I am the man on top, and I shall tell the people round me the truth."

" 'The massive Mr. Smith rose and went slowly to the window, but he spoke with equal firmness. "I must be sent down," he said, "and the people must not be told the truth."

" ' "And why not?" asked the other.

" i "Because I mean to follow your advice," answered the massive youth, in heavy meditation. "I mean to keep the remaining shots for people in the shameful state you and I were in last night—I wish we could even plead drunkenness. I mean to keep those bullets for pessimists—pills for pale people. And in this way I want to walk the world like a wonderful surprise—to float as idly as the thistledown, and come as silently as the sunrise; not to be expected any more than the thunderbolt, not to be recalled any more than the dying breeze. I don't want people to anticipate me as a well-known practical joke. I want both my gifts to come virgin and violent, the death and the life after death. I am going to hold a pistol to the head of the Modern Man. But I shall not use it to kill him. Only to bring him to life. I begin to see a new meaning in being the skeleton at the feast."

" ' "You can scarcely be called a skeleton," said Dr. Eames, smiling.

u l "That comes of being so much at the feast," answered the massive youth. "No skeleton can keep his figure if he is always dining out; but that is not quite w T hat I meant. What I mean is that I caught a kind of glimpse of the meaning of death and all that. The skull and cross-bones, the memento mori. It isn't only meant to remind us of a future life, but to remind us of a present life, too. With our weak spirits we should grow old in eternity, if we were not kept young by death. Providence has to cut immortality into lengths for us, as nurses cut the bread and butter into fingers."

" 'Then he added suddenly in a voice of unnatural actuality, "But I know something now, Eames. I knew it when the clouds turned pink."

"' "What do you mean?" asked Eames. "What did you know?"

" ' "I knew for the first time that murder is really wrong."

" 'He gripped Dr. Eames's hand and groped his way somewhat unsteadily to the door. Before he had vanished through it he had added, "It's very dangerous, though, when a man thinks for a split second that he understands death."

" 'Dr. Eames remained in repose and rumination some hours after his late assailant had left. Then he rose, took his hat and umbrella, and went for a brisk if rotatory walk. Several times, however, he stood outside the villas with the spotted blinds, studying them intently with his head slightly on one side. Some took him for a lunatic and some for an intending purchaser. He is no*, yet sure that the two characters would be widely different.

" 'The above narrative has been constructed on a principle which is (in the opinion of the undersigned persons) new in the art of

letters. Each of the two actors is described as he appeared to the other. But the undersigned persons absolutely guarantee the exactitude of the story; and if their version of the thing be questioned, they (the undersigned persons) would deucedly well like to know who does know ajpout it if they don't. " 'The undersigned persons will now adjourn to u The Spotted Dog" for beer. Farewell.

"' \'7bSigned) JAMES EMERSON EAMES, " 'Warden of Brakespeare College, Cambridge.

"'Innocent Smith.'"

## CHAPTER II

## THE TWO CURATES; OR, THE BURGLARY CHARGE

ARTHUR INGLEWOOD handed the document he had just read to the leaders of the prosecution, who examined it with their heads together. Both the Jew and the American were of sensitive and excitable stocks; and they revealed by the jumpings and bumpings of the black head and the yellow that nothing could be v a^ne in the way of denial of the document. The letter from the Warden was as authentic as the letter from the Sub-Warden, however regrettably different in dignity and social tone.

"Very few words," said l'n to iK K*$ "are required to conclude our case in mis' matter. Surely it is now plain that our client carried his pistol about with the eccentric but innocent purpose of giving a wholesome scare to those whom he regarded as blasphemers.

In each case the scare was so wholesome that the victim himself has dated from it as from a new birth. Smith, so far from being a madman, is rather a mad doctor—he walks the world curing frenzies and not distributing them. That is the answer to the two unanswerable questions which I put to the prosecutors. That is why they dared not produce a line by any one who had actually confronted the pistol. All who had actually confronted the pistol confessed that they had profited by it. That was why Smith, though a good shot, never hit anybody. He never hit anybody because he was a good shot. His mind was as clear of murder as his hands are of blood. This, I say, is the only possible explanation of these facts and of all the other facts. No one can possibly explain the Warden's conduct except by believing the Warden's story. Even Dr. Pym, who is a very factory of ingenious theories, could find no other theory to cover the case."

"There are promising perspectives in hypnotism and dual personality," said Dr. Cyrus Pym dreamily; "the science of criminology is in its infancy, and—"

"Infancy!" cried Moon, jerking his red pencil in the air with a gesture of enlightenment; "why, that explains it."

"I repeat," proceeded Inglewood, "that neither Dr. Pym nor any one else can account on any other theory but ours for the Warden's signature, for the shots missed and the witnesses missing."

The little Yankee had slipped to his feet with some return of a cock-fighting coolness. "The defence," he said, "omits a coldly colossal fact. They say we produce none of the actual victims. Wal, here is one victim, England's celebrated and stricken Warner. I reckon he is pretty well produced. And they suggest that all the outrages were followed by reconciliations. Wal, there's no flies on England's Warner; and he isn't reconciled much."

"My learned friend," said Moon, getting elaborately to his feet, "must remember that the science of shooting Dr. Warner is in its infancy. Dr. Warner would strike the idlest eye as one specially difficult to startle into any recognition of the glory of God. We admit that our client, in this one instance, failed, and that the operation was not successful. But I am empowered to offer, on behalf of my client, a proposal for operating on Dr. Warner again, at his earliest convenience, and without further fees."

" 'Ang it all, Michael," cried Gould, quite serious for the first time in his life; "you might give us a bit of bally sense for a chinge."

"What was Dr. Warner talking about just before the first shot?" asked Moon sharply.

"The creature," said Dr. Warner superciliously, "asked me, with characteristic rationality, whether it was my birthday."

"And you answered, with characteristic swank," cried Moon, shooting out a long lean finger as rigid and arresting as the pistol of Smith, "that you didn't keep your birthday."

"Something like that," assented the doctor.

"Then," continued Moon, "he asked you why not, and you said it was because you didn't see that birth was anything to rejoice over. Agreed? Now, is there any one who doubts that our tale is true?"

There was a cold crash of stillness in the room; and Moon said, "Pax populi vox dei; it is the silence of the people that is the voice of God; or in Dr. Pym's more civilized language, 'it is up to him to open the next change.' On this we claim an acquittal."

It was about an hour later. Dr. Cyrus Pym had remained for an unprecedented time with his eyes closed and this thumb and finger in the air. It almost seemed as if he had been "struck so," as the nurses say; and in the deathly silence Michael Moon felt forced to relieve the strain with some remark. For the last half-hour or so the eminent criminologist had been explaining that science took the same view of offences against property as it did of offences against life. "Most murder," he had said, "is a variation of homicidal mania, and in the same way most theft is a version of kleptomania. I cannot entertain any doubt that my learned friends opposite adequately conceive how this must involve a scheme of punishment more tol'rant and humane than the cruel methods of ancient codes. They will doubtless exhibit consciousness of a chasm so eminently yawning, so thought-arresting, so—" It was here that he paused and indulged in the delicate gesture to which allusion has been made; and Michael could bear it no longer.

"Yes, yes," he said impatiently, "we admit the chasm. The old cruel codes accused a man of theft and sent him to prison for ten years. The tolerant and humane ticket accuses him of nothing and sends him to prison for ever. We pass the chasm."

It was characteristic of the eminent Pym, in one of his trances of verbal fastidiousness, that he went on, unconscious not only of his opponent's interruption, but even of his own pause.

"So stock-improving," continued Dr. Cyrus Pym, "so fraught with real high hopes of the future. Science, therefore, regards thieves, in the abstract, just as it regards murderers. It regards them not as sinners to be punished for an arbitrary period, but as patients to be detained and cured for— n (his two first digits closed again as he hesitated) "in short, for the required period. But there is something special in the case we investigate here. Kleptomania commonly conjoins itself—"

"I beg pardon," said Michael; "I did not ask just now because, to tell the truth, I really thought our guest, though seemingly vertical, was enjoying well-earned slumber, with a pinch in his fingers of scentless and delicate dust. But now that things are moving a little more, there is something I should really like to know. I have hung on Dr. Pym's lips, of course, with an interest that it were weak to call rapture, but I have so far been unable to form any conjecture about what the accused, in the present instance, is supposed to have been and gone and done."

"If Mr. Moon will have patience," said Pym, with dignity, "he will find that this was the very point to which my exposition was directed. Kleptomania, I say, exhibits itself as a kind of physical attraction to certain defined materials; and it has been held (by no less a man than Harris) that this is the ultimate explanation of the strict specialism and vurry narrow professional outlook of most criminals. One will have an irresistible physical impulsion towards pearl sleeve-links, while he passes over the most elegant and celebrated diamond sleeve-links, placed about in the most conspicuous locations. Another will impede his flight with no less than forty-seven buttoned boots, while elastic-sided boots leave him cold, and even sarcastic. The specialism of the criminal, I repeat, is a mark rather of insanity than of any brightness of business habits; but there is one kind of depredator to whom this principle is at first sight hard to apply. I allude to our fellow-citizen the housebreaker.

"It has been maintained by some of our boldest young truth-seekers, that the eye of a burglar beyond the back-garden wall could hardly be caught and hypnotized by a fork that is insulated in a locked box under the butler's bed. They have thrown down the gauntlet to American science on this point. They declare that diamond links are not left about in conspicuous locations in the haunts of the lower classes, as they were in the great test experiment of Calypso College. We hope this experiment here will be an answer to that young ringing challenge, and will bring the burglar once more into line and union with his fellow criminals."

Moon, whose face had gone through every phase of black bewilderment for five minutes past, suddenly lifted his hand and struck the table in explosive enlightenment.

"Oh, I see!" he cried; "you mean that Smith is a burglar."

"I thought I made it quite ad'quately lucid," said Mr. Pym, folding up his eyelids. It was typical of this topsy-turvy private trial that all the eloquent extras, all the rhetoric or digression on either side was exasperating and unintelligible to the other. Moon could not make head or tail of the solemnity of a new civilization. Pym could not make head or tail of the gaiety of an old one.

"All the cases in which Smith has figured as an expropriator," continued the American doctor, "are cases of burglary. Pursuing the same course as in the previous case, we select the indubitable instance from the rest, and we take the most correct cast-iron evidence. I will now call on my colleague, Mr. Gould, to read a letter we have received from the earnest, unspotted Canon of Durham, Canon Hawkins."

Mr. Moses Gould leapt up with his usual alacrity to read the letter from the earnest and unspotted Hawkins. Moses Gould could imitate a farmyard well, Sir Henry Irving not so well, Marie Lloyd to a point of excellence, and the new motor horns in a manner that put him upon the platform of great artists. But his imitation of a Canon of Durham was not convincing; indeed, the sense of the letter was so much obscured by the extraordinary leaps and gasps of his pronunciation that it is perhaps better to print it here as Moon read it when, a little later, it was handed across the table.

"Dear Sir,—I can scarcely feel surprise that the incident you mention, private as it was, should have filtered through our omnivorous journals to the mere populace; for the position I have since attained makes me, I conceive, a public character, and this was certainly the most extraordinary incident in a not uneventful and perhaps not an undistinguished career. I am by no means without experience in scenes of civil tumult. I have faced many a political crisis in the old Primrose League days at Heme Bay, and, before I broke with the wilder set, have spent many a night at the Christian Social Union. But this other experience was quite inconceivable. I can only describe it as the letting loose of a place which it is not for me, as a clergyman, to mention.

"It occurred in the days when I was, for a short period, a curate at Hoxton; and the other curate, then my colleague, induced me to attend a meeting which he described, I must say profanely described, as calculated to promote the Kingdom of God. I found, on the contrary, that it consisted entirely of men in corduroys and greasy clothes whose manners were coarse and their opinions extreme.

"Of my colleague in question I wish to speak with the fullest respect and friendliness, and I will, therefore, say little. No one can be more convinced than I of the evil of politics in the pulpit; and I never offer my congregation any advice about voting except in cases in which I feel strongly that they are likely to make an erroneous selection. But, while I do not mean to touch at all upon political or social problems, I must say that for a clergyman to countenance, even in jest, such discredited nostrums of dissipated demagogues as Socialism or Radicalism partakes of the character of the betrayal of a sacred trust. Far be it from me to say a word against the Reverend Raymond Percy, the colleague in question. He was brilliant, I suppose, and to some apparently fascinating; but a clergyman who talks like a Socialist, wears his hair like a pianist, and behaves like an intoxicated person, will never rise in his profession, or even obtain the admiration of the good and wise. Nor is it for me to utter my personal judgments of the appearance of the people in the hall. Yet a glance round the room, revealing ranks of debased and envious faces—"

"Adopting," said Moon explosively, for he was getting restive, "adopting the reverend gentleman's favourite figure of logic, may I say that while tortures would not tear from me a whisper about his intellect, he is a blasted old jackass."

"Really!" said Dr. Pym; "I protest."

"You must keep quiet, Michael," said Ingle-wood; "they have a right to read their story."

"Chair! Chair! Chair!" cried Gould, rolling about exuberantly in his own; and Pym glanced for a moment towards the canopy which covered all the authority of the Court of Beacon.

"Oh, don't wake the old lady," said Moon, lowering his own voice in a moody good-humour. "I apologize. I won't interrupt again."

Before the little eddy of interruption was ended the reading of the clergyman's letter was already continuing.

"The proceedings opened with a speech from my colleague, of which I will say nothing. It was deplorable. Many of the audience were Irish, and showed the weakness of that impetuous people. When gathered together into gangs and conspiracies they seem to lose altogether that lovable good-nature and readiness to accept anything one tells them which distinguishes them as individuals."

With a slight start Michael rose to his feet, bowed solemnly, and sat down again.

"These persons, if not silent, were at least applausive during the speech of Mr. Percy. He descended to their level with witticisms about rent and a reserve of labour. Confisca- tion, expropriation, arbitration, and such words with which I cannot soil my lips recurred constantly. Some hours afterwards the storm broke. I had been addressing the meeting for some time, pointing out the lack of thrift in the working classes, their insufficient attendance at evening service, their neglect of the Harvest Festival, and of many other things that might materially help them to improve their lot. It was, I think, about this time that an extraordinary interruption occurred. An enormous, powerful man, partly concealed with white plaster, arose in the middle of the hall, and offered (in a loud, roaring voice, like a bull's) some observations which seemed to be in a foreign language. Mr. Raymond Percy, my colleague, descended to his level by entering into a duel of repartee, in which he appeared to be the victor. The meeting began to behave more respectfully for a little; yet before I had said twelve sentences more the rush was made for the platform. The enormous plasterer, in particular, plunged towards us, shaking the earth like an elephant; and I really do not know what would have happened if a man equally large, but not quite so ill-dressed, had not jumped up also and held him away. This other big man shouted a sort of speech to the mob as he was shoving them back. I don't know what he said, but, what with shouting and shoving and such horseplay, he got us out at a back door, while the wretched people went roaring down another passage.

"Then follows the truly extraordinary part of my story. When he had got us outside, in a mean backyard of blistered grass leading into a lane with a very lonely-looking lamp-post, this giant addressed us as follows: 'You're well out of that, sir; now you'd better come along with me. I want you to help me in an act of social justice, such as we've all been talking about. Come along!' And turning his big back abruptly, he led us down the lean old lane with the one lean old lamp-post, we scarcely knowing what to do but to follow him. He had certainly helped us in a most difficult situation, and, as a gentleman, I could not treat such a benefactor with suspicion without grave grounds. Such also was the view of my Socialistic colleague, who (with all his dreadful talk of arbitration) is a gentleman also. In fact, he comes of the Staffordshire Percys, a branch of the old house; and has the black hair and pale, clear-cut face of the whole family. I cannot but refer it to vanity that he should heighten his personal advantages with black velvet or a red cross of considerable ostentation, and certainly—but I digress.

"A fog was coming up the street, and that last lost lamp-post faded behind us in a way that certainly depressed the mind. The large man in front of us looked larger and larger in the haze. He did not turn round, but he said with his huge back to us, 'All that talk-ing's no good; we want a little practical Socialism.'

u 'I quite agree,' said Percy, 'but I always like to understand things in theory before I put them into practice.'

" ( Oh, you leave it to me,' said the practical Socialist, or whatever he was, with the most terrifying vagueness. 'I have a way with me. I'm a permeator.'

"I could not imagine what he meant, but my companion laughed, so I was sufficiently reassured to continue the unaccountable journey for the present. It led us through most singular ways; out of the lane, where we were already rather cramped, into a paved passage, at the end of which we passed through a wooden gate left open. We then found ourselves, in the increasing darkness and vapour, crossing what appeared to be a beaten path across a kitchen garden. I called out to the enormous person going on in front, but he answered obscurely that it was a short cut.

"I was just repeating my very natural doubt to my clerical companion when I was brought up against a short ladder, apparently leading to a higher level of road. My thoughtless colleague ran up it so quickly that I could not do otherwise than follow as best I could. The path on which I then planted my feet was quite unprecedentedly narrow. I had never had to walk along a thoroughfare so exiguous. Along one side of it grew what, in the dark and density of air, I first took to be some short, strong thicket of shrubs. Then I saw that they were not short shrubs; they were the tops of tall trees. I, an English gentleman and clergyman of the Church of England—I was walking along the top of a garden wall like a torn cat.

"I am glad to say that I stopped within my first five steps, and let loose my just reprobation, balancing myself as best I could all the time.

" 'It's a right-of-way/ declared my indefensible informant. 'It's closed to traffic once in a hundred years.'

" 'Mr. Percy, Mr. Percy!' I called out; 'you are not going on with this blackguard?'

" 'Why, I think so,' answered my unhappy colleague flippantly. 'I think you and I are bigger blackguards than he is, whatever he is.'

" 'I am a burglar,' explained the big creature quite calmly. 'I am a member of the Fabian Society. I take back the wealth stolen by the capitalist, not by sweeping civil war and revolution, but by reform fitted to the special occasion—here a little and there a little. Do you see that fifth house along the terrace with the flat roof? I'm permeating that one to-night.'

" 'Whether this is a crime or a joke,' I cried, 'I desire to be quit of it.'

" 'The ladder is just behind you,' answered the creature with horrible courtesy; 'and, before you go, do let me give you my card.'

"If I had had the presence of mind to show any proper spirit I should have flung it away, though any adequate gesture of the kind would have gravely affected my equilibrium upon the wall. As it was, in the wildness of the moment, I put it in my waistcoat pocket, and, picking my way back by wall and ladder, landed in the respectable streets once more. Not before, however, I had seen with my own eyes the two awful and lamentable facts—that the burglar was climbing up a slanting roof towards the chimneys, and that Raymond Percy—a priest of God and, what was worse, a gentleman—was crawling up after him. I have never seen either of them since that day.

"In consequence of this soul-searching experience I severed my connection with the wild set. I am far from saying that every member of the Christian Social Union must necessarily be a burglar. I have no right to bring any such charge. But it gave me a hint of what such courses may lead to in many cases; and I saw them no more.

"I have only to add that the photograph you enclose, taken by a Mr. Inglewood, is undoubtedly that of the burglar in question. When I got home that night I looked at his card, and he was inscribed there under the name of Innocent Smith.—Yours faithfully, "John Clement Hawkins."

Moon merely went through the form of glancing at the paper. He knew that the prosecutors could not have invented so heavy a document; that Moses Gould (for one) could no more write like a canon than he could read like one. After handing it back he rose to open the defence on the burglary charge.

"We wish," said Michael, "to give all reasonable facilities to the prosecution; especially as it will save the time of the whole court. The latter object I shall once again pursue by passing over all those points of theory which are so dear to Dr. Pym. I know how they are made. Perjury is a variety of aphasia, leading a man to say one thing instead of another. Forgery is a kind of writer's cramp, forcing a man to write his uncle's name instead of his own. Piracy on the high seas is probably a form of seasickness. But it is unnecessary for us to inquire into the causes of a fact which we deny. Innocent Smith never did commit burglary at all.

"I should like to claim the power permitted by our previous arrangement, and ask the prosecution two or three questions."

Dr. Cyrus Pym closed his eyes to indicate a courteous assent.

"In the first place," continued Moon, "have you the date of Canon Hawkins's last glimpse of Smith and Percy climbing up the walls and roofs?"

"Ho, yuss!" called out Gould smartly. "November thirteen, eighteen ninety-one."

"Have you," continued Moon, "identified the houses in Hoxton up which they climbed?"

"Must have been Ladysmith Terrace out of Hoxton High Road," answered Gould with the same clockwork readiness.

"Well," said Michael, cocking an eyebrow at him, "was there any burglary in that terrace that night? Surely you could find that out."

"There may well have been," said the doctor primly after a pause, "an unsuccessful one that led to no legalities."

"Another question," proceeded Michael. "Canon Hawkins, in his blood-and-thunder boyish way, left off at the exciting moment. Why don't you produce the evidence of the other clergyman, who actually followed the burglar and presumably was present at the crime?"

Dr. Pym rose and planted the points of his fingers on the table as he did when he was specially confident of the clearness of his reply.

"We have entirely failed," he said, "to track the other clergyman, who seems to have melted into the ether after Canon Hawkins had seen him ascending the gutters and the leads. I am fully aware that this may strike many as sing'lar; yet, upon reflection, I think it will appear pretty natural to a bright thinker. This Mr. Raymond Percy is admittedly, by the canon's evidence, a minister of eccentric ways. His connection with England's proudest and fairest does not seemingly prevent a taste for the society of the real low-down. On the other hand, the prisoner Smith is, by general agreement, a man of irresistible fascination. I entertain no doubt that Smith led the Reverend Percy into the crime and forced him to hide his head in the real criminal class. That would fully account for his nonappearance, and the failure of all attempts to trace him."

"It is impossible, then, to trace him?" asked Moon.

"Impossible," repeated the specialist, shutting his eyes.

"You are sure it is impossible?"

"Oh, dry up, Michael," cried Gould, irritably; "we'd 'ave found 'im if we could, for you bet 'e saw the burglary. Don't you start looking for 'im. Look for your own 'ead in the dustbin. You'll find that—after a bit," and his voice died away in grumbling.

"Arthur," directed Michael Moon, sitting down. "Kindly read Mr. Raymond Percy's letter to the court."

"Wishing, as Mr. Moon has said, to shorten the proceedings as much as possible," began Inglewood, "I will not read the first part of the letter sent to us. It is only fair to the prosecution to admit the account given by the second clergyman fully ratifies, as far as facts are concerned, that given by the first clergyman. We concede, then, the canon's story so far as it goes. This must necessarily be valuable to the prosecutor and also convenient to the court. I begin Mr. Percy's letter then, at 206

the point when all three men were standing on the garden wall,—

" 'As I watched Hawkins wavering on the wall, I made up my own mind not to waver. A cloud of wrath was on my brain, like the cloud of copper fog on the houses and gardens round. My decision was violent and simple; yet the thoughts that led up to it were so complicated and contradictory that I could not retrace them now. I knew Hawkins was a kind, innocent gentleman; and I would have given ten pounds for the pleasure of kicking him down the road. That God should allow good people to be as bestially stupid as that— rose against me like a towering blasphemy.

" 'At Oxford, I fear, I had the artistic temperament rather badly; and artists love to be limited. I liked the church as a pretty pattern; discipline was mere decoration. I delighted in mere divisions of time; I liked eating fish on Friday. But then I like fish; and the fast was made for men who like meat. Then I came to Hoxton and found men who had fasted for five hundred years; men who 207

had to gnaw fish because they could not get meat—and fish-bones when they could not get fish. As too many British officers treat the army as a review, so I had treated the Church Militant as if it were the Church Pageant. Hoxton cures that. Then I realized that for eighteen hundred years the Church Militant had been not a pageant, but a riot—and a suppressed riot. There, still living patiently in Hoxton, were people to whom the tremendous promises had been made. In the face of that I had to become revolutionary if I was to continue to be religious. In Hoxton one cannot be a conservative without being also an atheist —and a pessimist. Nobody but the devil could want to conserve Hoxton.

" 'On the top of all this comes Hawkins. If he had cursed all the Hoxton men, excommunicated them and told them they were going to hell, I should have rather admired him. If he had ordered them all to be burned in the market-place, I should still have had that patience that all good Christians have with the wrongs inflicted on other people. But there is no priestcraft about Hawkins—nor any other kind of craft. He is as perfectly incapable of being a priest as he is of being a carpenter or a cabman or a gardener or a plasterer. He is a perfect gentleman; that is his complaint. He does not impose his creed, but simply his class. He never said a word of religion in the whole of his damnable address. He simply said all the things his brother, the major, would have said. A voice from heaven assures me that he has a brother, and that this brother is a major.

11 'When this helpless aristocrat had praised cleanliness in the body and convention in the soul to people who could hardly keep body and soul together, the stampede against our platform began. I took part in his undeserved rescue, I followed his obscure deliverer, until (as I have said) we stood together on the wall above the dim gardens, already clouding with fog. Then I looked at the curate and at the burglar, and decided, in a spasm of inspiration, that the burglar was the better man of the two. The burglar seemed quite as kind and human as the curate was—and he was also brave and self-reliant, which the curate was not. I knew there was no virtue in the upper class, for I belong to it myself; I knew there was not so very much in the lower class, for I had lived with it a long time. Many old texts about the despised and persecuted came back to my mind; and I thought that the saints might well be hidden in the criminal class. About the time Hawkins let himself down the ladder I was crawling up a low, sloping, blue-slate roof after the large man, who went leaping in front of me like a gorilla.

" 'This upward scramble was short, and we soon found ourselves tramping along a broad road of flat roofs, broader than many big thoroughfares, with chimney-pots here and there that seemed in the haze as bulky as small forts. The asphyxiation of the fog seemed to increase the somewhat swollen and morbid anger under which my brain and body laboured. The sky and all those things that are commonly clear seemed overpowered by sinister spirits. Tall spectres with turbans of vapour seemed to stand higher than sun or moon, eclipsing both. I thought dimly of illustrations to the "Arabian Nights" on brown paper with rich but sombre tints, showing genii gathering round the Seal of Solomon. By the way, what was the Seal of Solomon? Nothing to do with sealing-wax really, I suppose; but my muddled fancy felt the thick clouds as being of that heavy and clinging substance, of strong opaque colour, poured out of boiling pots and stamped into monstrous emblems.

" 'The first effect of the tall turbaned vapours was that discoloured look of pea soup or coffee brown of which Londoners commonly speak. But the scene grew subtler with familiarity. We stood above the average of the housetops and saw something of that thing called smoke, which in great cities creates the strange thing called fog. Beneath us rose a forest of chimney-pots. And there stood in every chimney-pot, as if it were a flower-pot, a brief shrub or a tall tree of coloured vapour. The colours of the smoke were various; for some chimneys were from firesides and some from factories and some again from mere rubbish heaps. And yet, though the tints were all varied, they all seemed unnatural, like fumes from a witch's pot. It was as if the shameful and ugly shapes growing shapeless in the cauldron sent up each its separate spurt of steam, coloured according to the fish or flesh consumed. Here, aglow from underneath, 211

MANALIVE

were dark red clouds, such as might drift from dark jars of sacrificial blood; there the vapour was dark indigo gray, like the long hair of witches steeped in the hell-broth. In another place the smoke was of an awful opaque ivory yellow, such as might be the disembodiment of one of their old, leprous, waxen images. But right across it ran a line of bright, sinister, sulphurous green, as clear and crooked as Arabic—'"

Mr. Moses Gould once more attempted the arrest of the bus. He was understood to suggest that the reader should shorten the proceedings by leaving out all the adjectives. Mrs. Duke, who had woken up, observed that she was sure it was all very nice, and the decision was duly noted down by Moses with a blue, and by Michael with a red, pencil. Inglewood then resumed the reading of the document.

11 Then I read the writing of the smoke. Smoke was like the modern city that makes it; it is not always dull or ugly, but it is always wicked and vain.

" 'Modern England was like a cloud of

MAN ALIVE

smoke; it could carry all colours, but it could leave nothing but a stain. It was our weakness and not our strength, that put a rich refuse in the sky. These were the rivers of our vanity pouring into the void. We had taken the sacred circle of the whirlwind, and looked down on it, and seen it as a whirlpool. And then we had used it as a sink. It was a good symbol of the mutiny in my own mind. Only our worst things were going to heaven. Only our criminals could still ascend like angels.

" 'As my brain was blinded with such emotions, my guide stopped by one of the big chimney-pots that stood at regular intervals like lamp-posts along that uplifted and aerial highway. He put his heavy hand upon it, and for the moment I thought he was merely leaning on it, tired with his steep scramble and long tramp along the top of the terrace. So far as I could guess from the abysses, full of fog on either side, and the veiled lights of red brown and old gold glowing through them now and again, we were on the top of one of those long, consecutive, and genteel rows of houses which are still to be found lifting their heads above poorer districts, the remains of 213

MANALI VE

tome rage of optimism in earlier speculative builders. Probably enough, they were entirely untenanted, or tenanted only by such small clans of the poor, as gather also in the old emptied palaces of Italy. Indeed, sometime later, when the fog had lifted a little, I discovered that we were walking round a semicircle of crescent which fell away below us into one flat square or wide street, below another like a giant stairway, in a manner not unknown in the eccentric building of London, and looking like the last ledges of the land. But a cloud sealed the giant stairway as yet.

" 'My speculations about the sullen skyscape, however, were interrupted by something as unexpected as the moon fallen from the sky. Instead of my burglar lifting his hand from the chimney he leaned on, he leaned on it a little more heavily, and the whole chimney-pot turned over like the opening top of an inkstand. I remembered the short ladder leaning against the low wall, and felt sure he had arranged his criminal approach long before.

" The collapse of the big chimney-pot ought to have been the culmination of my chaotic feelings; but, to tell the truth, it produced a sudden sense of comedy and even of comfort. I could not recall what connected this abrupt bit of housebreaking with some quaint but still kindly fancies. Then I remembered the delightful and uproarious scenes of roofs and chimneys in the harlequinades of my childhood, and was darkly, and quite irrationally comforted by a sense of unsubstantiality in the scene; as if the houses were of lath and paint and pasteboard, and were only meant to be tumbled in and out of by policemen and pantaloons. The law-breaking of my companion seemed not only seriously excusable, but even comically excusable. Who were all these pompous preposterous people with their footmen and their foot-scrapers, their chimney-pots and their chimney-pot hats, that they should prevent a poor clown from getting sausages if he wanted them? One would suppose that property was a serious thing. I had reached, as it were, a higher level of that mountain of vaporous visions; the heaven of a higher levity.

u 'My guide had jumped down into the dark cavity revealed by the displaced chimney-pot. He must have landed at a level considerably lower, for, tall as he was, nothing but his weirdly-tousled head remained visible. Something again far off, and yet familiar, pleased me about this way of invading the houses of men. I thought of little chimneysweeps, and "The Water Babies"; but I decided that it was not that. Then I remembered what it was that made me connect such topsyturvy trespass with ideas quite opposite to the idea of crime. Christmas Eve, of course, and Santa Claus coming down the chimney.

" 'Almost at the same instant the hairy head disappeared into the black hole; but I heard a voice calling to me from below. A second or two afterwards, the hairy head reappeared; it was dark against the more fiery part of the fog, and nothing could be spelt of its expression, but its voice called on me to follow with that enthusiastic impatience, proper only among old friends. I jumped into the gulf, and as blindly as Curtius, for I was still thinking of Santa Claus, and the traditional virtue of such vertical entrance.

" 'In every well-appointed gentleman's house, I reflected, there was the front door for the gentleman, and the side door for the tradesmen; but there was also the top door for the gods. The chimney is, so to speak, the underground passage between earth and heaven. By this starry tunnel Santa Claus manages—like the skylark—to be true to the kindred points of heaven and home. Nay, owing to certain conventions, and a widely distributed lack of courage for climbing, this door was, perhaps, little used. But Santa Claus's door was really the front door: it was the door fronting the universe.

" *I thought this as I groped my way across the black garret or loft below the roof and scrambled down the squat ladder that let us down into a yet larger loft below. Yet it was not till I was half-way down the ladder that I suddenly stood still, and thought for an instant of retracing all my steps, as my companion had retraced them from the beginning of the garden wall. The name of Santa Claus had suddenly brought me back to my senses. I remembered why Santa Claus came, and why he was welcome.

" 'I was brought up in the propertied classes, and with all their horror of offences against property. I had heard all the regular denuneiations of robbery, both right and wrong; I had read the Ten Commandments in church a thousand times. And then and there, at the age of thirty-four, half-way down a ladder in a dark room in the bodily act of burglary, I saw suddenly for the first time that theft, after all, is really wrong.

11 'It was too late to turn back, however, and I followed the strangely-soft footsteps of my huge companion across the lower and larger loft, till he knelt down on a part of the bare flooring and, after a few fumbling efforts, lifted a sort of trap-door. This released a light from below, and we found ourselves looking down into a lamp-lit sitting-room, of the sort that in large houses often leads out of a bedroom, and is an adjunct to it. Light thus breaking from beneath our feet like a soundless explosion, showed that the trap-door just lifted was clogged with dust and rust; and had doubtless been long disused until the advent of my enterprising friend. But I did not look at this long, for the sight of the shining room underneath us had an almost unnatural attractiveness. To enter a modern interior at so strange an angle, by so forgotten a door,

*&*
N
'fe 9

"he knelt down on a part of the bare flooring and lifted a sort of trap door"
— Pagt 218

MANALIVE
was an epoch in one's psychology. It was like having found a fourth dimension.

11 'My companion dropped from the aperture into the room so suddenly and soundlessly, that I could do nothing but follow him; though, through lack of practice in crime, I was by no means soundless. Before the echo of my boots had died away, the big burglar had gone quickly to the door, half opened it, and stood looking down the staircase and listening. Then, leaving the door still half open, he came back into the middle of the room, and ran his roving blue eye round its furniture and ornament. The room was comfortably lined with books in that rich and human way that makes the walls seem alive; it was a deep and full, but slovenly, bookcase, of the sort that is constantly ransacked for. the purposes of reading in bed. One of those stunted German stoves that look like red goblins stood in a corner, and a sideboard of walnut wood, with closed doors in its lower part. There were three windows, high but narrow. After another glance round, my housebreaker plucked the walnut doors open and rummaged inside. He found nothing

there, apparently, except an extremely handsome cut-glass decanter, containing what looked like port. Somehow the sight of the thief returning with this ridiculous little luxury in his hand, woke within me once more all the revelation and revulsion I had felt above.

"*"Don't do it!" I cried quite incoherently. "Santa Claus—"

"'"Ah," said the burglar, as he put the decanter on the table and stood looking at me, "you've thought about that, too."

"'"I can't express a millionth part of what I've thought of," I cried, "but something like this ... oh, can't you see it? Why are children not afraid of Santa Claus, though he comes like a thief in the night? He is permitted secrecy, trespass, almost treachery—because there are more toys where he has been. What should we feel if there were less? Down what chimney from hell would come the goblin that should take away the children's balls and dolls while they slept? Could a Greek tragedy be more gray and cruel than that daybreak and awakening? Dog-stealer, horse-stealer, man-stealer—can you think of anything so base as a toy-stealer?"

"'The burglar, as if absently, took a large revolver from his pocket and laid it on the table beside the decanter, but still kept his blue reflective eyes fixed on my face.

"■"Man!" I said, "all stealing is toy-stealing. That's why it's really wrong. The goods of the unhappy children of men should be respected because of their worthlessness. I know Naboth's vineyard is as painted as Noah's Ark. I know Nathan's ewe-lamb is really a woolly baa-lamb on a wooden stand. That is why I could not take them away. I did not mind so much, as long as I thought of men's things as their valuables; but I dare not put a hand upon their vanities."

"'After a moment I added abruptly, "Only saints and sages ought to be robbed. They may be stripped and pillaged; but not the poor little worldly people of the things that are their poor little pride."

11 'He set out two wine-glasses from the cupboard, filled them both, and lifted one of them with a salutation towards his lips.

"«"Don't do it!" I cried. "It might be the last bottle of some rotten vintage or other. The master of this house may be proud of it. Don't you see there's something sacred in the silliness of such things?"

"'"It's not the last bottle," answered my criminal calmly, "there's plenty more in the cellar."

" c "You know the house, then?" I said.

" c "Too well," he answered, with a sadness so strange as to have something eerie about it. "I am always trying to forget what I know— and to find what I don't know." He drained his glass. "Besides," he added, "it will do him good."

"'"What will do him good?"

"""The wine I'm drinking," said the strange person.

" c "Does he drink too much, then?" I inquired.

"'"No," he answered; "not unless I do."

"("Do you mean," I demanded, "that the owner of this house approves of all you do?"

"l"God forbid," he answered; "but he has to do the same."

"'The dead face of the fog looking in at all

the three windows unreasonably increased a sense of riddle, and even terror, about this tall, narrow house we had entered out of the sky. I had once more the notion about the gigantic genii—I fancied that enormous Egyptian faces, of the dead reds and yellows of Egypt, were staring in at each window of our little lamp-lit room as at a lighted stage of marionettes. My companion went on playing with the pistol in front of him, and talking with the same rather creepy confi-dentialness.

u ' "I am always trying to find him—to catch him unawares. I come in through skylights and trap-doors to find him; but whenever I find him—he is doing what I am doing."

11 'I sprang to my feet with a thrill of fear. "There is some one coming," I cried, and my cry had something of a shriek in it.

" 'Not from the stairs below, but along the passage from the inner bedchamber (which seemed somehow to make it more alarming), footsteps were coming nearer. I am quite unable to say what mystery, or monster, or double, I expected to see when the door was pushed open from within. I am only quite certain that I did not expect to see what I did see.

44 'Framed in the open doorway stood, with an air of great serenity, a rather tall young woman, definitely, but indefinably artistic— her dress the colour of spring and her hair of autumn leaves, with a face which, though still comparatively young, conveyed experience as well as intelligence. All she said was, "I didn't hear you come in."

14 ' "I came in another way," said the per-meator, somewhat vaguely. "I'd left my latchkey at home."

44 'I got to my feet in a mixture of politeness and mania. "I'm really very sorry," I cried. "I know my position is irregular. Would you be so obliging as to tell me whose house this is?"

" 444 Mine," said the burglar. "May I present you to my wife?"

" 'I doubtfully, and somewhat slowly, resumed my seat; and I did not get out of it till nearly morning. Mrs. Smith (such was the prosaic name of this far from prosaic household) lingered a little, talking slightly and pleasantly. She left on my mind the impression of a certain odd mixture of shyness and sharpness; as if she knew the world well, but was still a little harmlessly afraid of it. Perhaps the possession of so jumpy and incalculable a husband had left her a little nervous. Anyhow, when she had retired to the inner chamber once more, that extraordinary man poured forth his apologia and autobiography over the dwindling wine. " 'He had been sent to Cambridge with a view to a mathematical and scientific, rather than a classical or literary, career. A starless nihilism was then the philosophy of the schools; and it bred in him a war between the members and the spirit, but one in which the members were right. While his brain accepted the black creed, his very body rebelled against it. As he put it, his right hand taught him terrible things. As the authorities of Cambridge University put it, unfortunately it had taken the form of his right hand flourishing a loaded firearm in the very face of a distinguished don, and driving him to climb out of the window and cling to a waterspout. He had done it solely because the poor don had professed in theory a preference for non-existence. For this very unacademic type of argument he had been sent down, vomiting as he was with revulsion, from the pessimism that had quailed under his pistol, he made himself a kind of fanatic of the joy of life. He cut across all the associations of serious-minded men. He was gay, but by no means careless. His practical jokes were more in earnest than verbal ones. Though not an optimist, in the absurd sense of maintaining that life is all beer and skittles, he did really seem to maintain that beer and skittles are the most serious part of it. "What is more immortal," he would cry, "than love and war? Type of all desire and joy—beer. Type of all battle and conquest—skittles."

" 'There was something in him of what the Old World called the solemnity of revels—when they spoke of "solemnizing" a mere masquerade or wedding banquet. Nevertheless, he was not a mere pagan any more than he was a mere practical joker. His eccentricities sprang from a static fact of faith, in itself mystical, and even childlike, and Christian.

I don't deny," he said, "that there should be priests to remind men that they will one day die. I only say that at certain strange epochs it is necessary to have another kind of priests, called poets, actually to remind men that they are not dead yet. The intellectuals among whom I moved were not even alive enough to fear death. They hadn't blood enough in them to be cowards. Until a pistol-barrel was poked under their very noses they never even knew they had been born. For ages looking up an eternal perspective it might be true that life is a learning to die. But for these little white rats it was just as true that death was their only chance of learning to live."

" 'His creed of wonder was Christian by this absolute test; that he felt it continually slipping from himself as much as from others. He had the same pistol for himself, as Brutus said of the dagger. He continually ran preposterous risks of high precipice or headlong speed to keep alive the mere conviction that he was alive. He treasured up trivial and yet insane details that had once reminded him of the awful subconscious reality. When the don had hung on the stone gutter, the sight of his long dangling legs, vibrating in the void like wings, somehow awoke the naked satire of the old definition of man as, a two-legged animal without feathers. The wretched professor had been brought into peril by his head, which he had so elaborately cultivated, and only saved by his legs, which he had treated with coldness and neglect. Smith could think of no other way of announcing or recording this, except to send a telegram to an old school friend (by this time a total stranger) to say that he had just seen a man with two legs; and that the man was alive.

" 'The uprush of his released optimism burst into stars like a rocket when he suddenly fell in love. He happened to be shooting a high and very headlong weir in a canoe, by way of proving to himself that he was alive; and he soon found himself involved in some doubt about the continuance of the fact. What was worse, he found he had equally jeopardized a harmless lady alone in a rowing boat, and one who had provoked death by no professions of philosophic negation. He apologized in wild gasps through all his wild wet labours to bring her to the shore, and when he had done so at last, he seems to have proposed to her on the bank. Anyhow, with the same impetuosity w r ith which he had nearly murdered her, he completely married her; and she was the lady in green to whom I had recently said "good-night."

14 They had settled down in these high narrow houses near Highbury. Perhaps, indeed, that is hardly the word. One could strictly say that Smith was married, that he was very happily married, that he not only did not care for any woman but his wife, but did not seem to care for any place but his home; but perhaps one could hardly say that he had settled down. "I am a very domestic fellow," he explained with gravity, "and I have often come in through a broken window

rather than be late for tea."

" 'He lashed his soul with laughter to prevent it falling asleep. He lost his wife a series of excellent servants by knocking at the door as a total stranger, and asking if Mr. Smith lived there and what kind of a man he was. The London general servant is not used to the master indulging in such transcendental ironies; and it was found impossible to explain to her that he did it in order to feel the same interest in his own affairs that he always felt in other people's.

"' "I know there's a fellow called Smith," he said in his rather weird way, "living in one of the tall houses in this terrace. I know he is really happy, and yet I can never catch him at it."

" 'Sometimes he would, of a sudden, treat his wife with a kind of paralyzed politeness, like a young stranger struck with love at first sight. Sometimes he would extend this poetic fear to the very furniture; would seem to apologize to the chair he sat on, and climb the staircase as cautiously as a cragsman, to renew in himself the sense of their skeleton of reality. Every stair is a ladder and every stool a leg, he said. And at other times he would play the stranger exactly in the opposite sense, and would enter by another way, so as to feel like a thief and a robber. He would break and violate his own home, as he had done with me that night. It was nearly morning before I could tear myself from this queer confidence of the Man Who Would Not Die, and as I shook hands with him on the doorsteps the last load of fog was lifting, and rifts of daylight revealed the stairway of irregular street levels that looked like the end of the world.

" 'It will be enough for many to say that I had passed a night with a maniac. What other term, it will be said, could he applied to such a being? A man who reminds himself that he is married by pretending not to be married! A man who tries to covet his own goods instead of his neighbours! On this I have but one word to say, and I feel it of my honour to say it, though no one understands. I believe the maniac was one of those who do not merely come, but are sent; sent like a great gale upon ships by Him who made His angels winds and His messengers a flaming fire. This, at least, I know for certain. Whether such men have laughed or wept, we have laughed at their laughter as much as at their weeping. Whether they cursed or blessed the world, they have never fitted it. It is true that men have shrunk from the sting of a great satirist as if from the sting of an adder. But it is equally true that men flee from the embrace of a great optimist as from the embrace of a bear. Nothing brings down more curses than a real benediction. For the goodness of good things, like the badness of bad things, is a prodigy past speech; it is to be pictured rather than spoken. We shall have gone deeper than the deeps of heaven and grown older than the oldest angels before we feel, even in its first faint vibrations, the everlasting violence of that double passion with which God hates and loves the world.—I am, yours faithfully, " 'Raymond Percy.* "

"Oh! 'Oly, 'Oly, 'Oly!" said Mr. Moses Gould.

The instant he had spoken all the rest knew they had been in an almost religious state of submission and assent. Something had bound them all together; something in the sacred tradition of the last two words of the letter; something also in the touching and boyish embarrassment with which Inglewood had read them—for he had all the thin-skinned reverence of the agnostic. Moses Gould was as good a fellow in his way as ever lived; far kinder to his family than more refined men of pleasure, simple and steadfast in his admirations, a thoroughly wholsesome animal and a thoroughly genuine character. But wherever there is conflict crises come in which any soul, personal or racial, unconsciously turns on the world the most hateful of its hundred faces. English reverence, Irish mysticism, American idealism, looked up and saw on the face of Moses a certain smile. It was that smile of the cynic triumphant which has been the tocsin for many a cruel riot in Russian villages of mediaeval towns.

"Oh! 'Oly, 'Oly, 'Oly!" said Moses Gould.

Finding that this was not well received, he explained further, exuberance deepening on his dark exuberant features.

"Always fun to see a bloke swallow a wasp when 'e's corfin' up a fly," he said pleasantly, "Don't you see youVe bunged up old Smith anyhow. If this parson's tale's O.K.—why, Smith is 'ot. 'E's pretty 'ot, we find him elopin' with Miss Gray (best respects!) in a cab. Well, what abart this Mrs. Smith the curate talks of, with her blarsted shyness— transmigogrified into a blighted sharpness.

Miss Gray ain't been very sharp, but I reckon 9he'll be pretty shy."

"Don't be a brute," growled Michael Moon.

None could lift their eyes to look at Mary; but Inglewood sent a glance along the table at Innocent Smith. He was still bowed above his paper toys, and a wrinkle was on his forehead that might have been worry or shame. He carefully plucked out one corner of a complicated paper strip and tucked it in elsewhere; then the wrinkle vanished and he looked relieved.

## CHAPTER III
## THE ROUND ROAD; OR, THE DESERTION CHARGE

PYM rose with sincere embarrassment; for he was an American, and his respect for ladies was real, and not at all scientific.

"Ignoring," he said, "the delicate and considerably knightly protests that have been called forth by my colleague's native sense of oration, and apologizing to all for whom our wild search for truth seems unsuitable to the grand ruins of a feudal land, I still think my colleague's question by no means devoid of relVancy. The last charge against the accused was one of burglary; the next charge on the paper is of bigamy and desertion. It does without question appear that the defence, in aspiring to rebut the last charge, have really admitted the next. Either Innocent Smith is still under a charge of attempted burglary, or else that is exploded; but he is pretty well fixed for attempted bigamy. It all depends what view we take of the alleged letter from Curate Percy. Under these conditions I feel justified in claiming my right to questions. May I ask how the defence got hold of the letter from Curate Percy? Did it come direct from the prisoner?"

"We have had nothing direct from the prisoner," said Moon quietly. "The two documents which the defence guarantees came to us from another quarter."

"From what quarter?" asked Dr. Pym.

"If you insist," answered Moon, "we had them from Miss Gray."

Dr. Cyrus Pym quite forgot to close his eyes, and, instead, opened them very wide.

"Do you really mean to say," he said, "that Miss Gray was in possession of this document testifying to a previous Mrs. Smith?"

"Quite so," said Inglewood, and sat down.

The doctor said something about infatuation in a low and painful voice, and then with visible difficulty continued his opening remarks.

"Unfortunately, the tragic truth revealed by Curate Percy's narrative is only too crushingly confirmed by other and monstrous documents in our possession. Of these the principal and most certain is the testimony of Innocent Smith's gardener, who was present at the most dramatic and eye-opening of his many acts of marital infidelity. Mr. Gould, the gardener, please."

Mr. Gould, with his tireless cheerfulness, arose to present the gardener. That functionary explained that he had served Mr. and Mrs. Innocent Smith when they had a little house on the edge of Croydon. From the gardener's tale, with its many small allusions, Inglewood grew certain that he had seen the place. It was one of those corners of town or country that one does not forget, for it looked like a frontier. The garden hung very high above the lane, and its end was steep and sharp, like a fortress. Beyond was a roll of real country, with a white path sprawling across it, and the roots, boles, and branches of great gray trees writhing and hoisting against the sky. But as if to assert that the lane itself was suburban, were sharply relieved against that gray and tossing upland a lamp-post painted a peculiar yellow-green and a red pillar-box that stood exactly at the corner.

Inglewood was sure of the place; he had passed it twenty times in his constitutionals on the bicycle; he had always dimly felt it was a place where something might occur. But it gave him quite a shiver to feel that the face of his frightful friend, or enemy, Smith, might at any time have appeared over the garden bushes above. The gardener's account, unlike the curate's, was quite free from decorative adjectives, however many he may have uttered privately while writing it. He simply said that on a particular morning Mr. Smith came out and began to play about with a rake, as he often did. Sometimes he would tickle the nose of his eldest child (he had two children); sometimes he would hook the rake on to the branch of a tree, and hoist himself up with horrible gymnastic jerks, like those of a giant frog in its final agony. Never, apparently, did he think of putting the rake to any of its proper uses, and the gardener, in consequence, treated his actions with coldness and brevity. But the gardener was certain that on one particular morning in October he (the gardener) had come round the corner of the house carrying the hose, had seen Mr. Smith standing on the lawn in a striped red and white jacket (which might have been his smoking jacket, but was quite as like a part of his pyjamas), and had heard him then and there call out to his wife, who was looking out of the bedroom window on to the garden, these decisive and very loud expressions,—

"I won't stay here any longer. I've got another wife and much better children a long way from here. My other wife's got redder hair than yours, and my other garden's got a much finer situation; and I'm going off to them."

With these words, apparently, he sent the rake flying far into the sky, higher than many could have shot an arrow, and caught it again. Then he cleared the hedge at a leap, and alighted on his feet down in the lane below, and set off up the road without even a hat. Much of the picture was doubtless supplied by Inglewood's accidental memory of the place. He could see with his mind's eye that big bare-headed figure with the ragged rake swaggering up the crooked woodland road, and leaving lamp-post and pillar-box behind.

But the gardener, on his own account, was quite prepared to swear to the public confession of bigamy, to the temporary disappearance of the rake in the sky, and the final disappearance of the man up the road. Moreover (being a local man) he could swear that, beyond some local rumours that Smith had embarked on the southeastern coast, nothing was known of him again.

This impression was somewhat curiously clinched by Michael Moon in the few but clear phrases in which he opened the defence upon the third charge. So far from denying that Smith had fled from Croydon and disappeared upon the Continent, he seemed prepared to prove all this on his own account. "I hope you are not so insular," he said, "that you will not respect the word of a French innkeeper as much as that of an English gardener. By Mr. Inglewood's favour we will hear the French innkeeper."

Before the company had decided the delicate point, Inglewood was already reading out the account in question. It was in French. It seemed to them to run something like this,—

"SIR,—Yes; I am Durobin of Durobin's Cafe on the sea-front at Gras, rather north of Dunquerque. I am willing to write all I know of the stranger out of the sea.

"I have no sympathy with eccentrics or poets. A man of sense looks for beauty in things deliberately intended to be beautiful, such as a trim flower-bed or an ivory statuette. One does not permit beauty to pervade one's whole life, just as one does not pave all the roads with ivory or cover all the fields with geraniums. My faith, but we should miss the onions!

"But whether I read things backwards through my memory, or whether there are indeed atmospheres of psychology which the eye of science cannot as yet pierce, it is the humiliating fact that on that particular evening I felt like a poet, like any little rascal of a poet who drinks absinthe in the mad Mont-mart re.

"Positively the sea itself looked like absinthe, green and bitter and poisonous. I had never known it look unfamiliar before. In the sky was that early and stormy darkness that is so depressing to the mind; and the wind blew shrilly round the little, lonely, coloured kiosk where they sell the newspapers, and along the sand-hills by the shore. Then I saw a fishing-boat with a brown sail standing in silently from the sea. It was already quite close, and out of it clambered a man of monstrous stature, who came wading to shore with the water not up to his knees, though it would have reached the hips of many men. He leaned on a long rake or forked pole, which looked like a trident, and made him look like a Triton. Wet as he was, and with strips of seaweed clinging to him, he walked across to my cafe, and, sitting down at a table outside, asked for sherry brandy, a liqueur which I keep, but is seldom demanded. Then the monster, with great politeness, invited me to partake of a vermouth before my dinner, and we fell into conversation. He had, apparently, crossed from Kent by a small boat, got at a private bargain because of some odd fancy he had for passing promptly in an easterly direction, and not waiting for any of the official boats. He was, he somewhat vaguely explained, looking for a house. When I naturally asked where the house was, he answered that he did not know; it was on an island; it was somewhere to the east; or, as he expressed it with a hazy and yet impatient gesture, 'over there.'

"I asked him how, if he did not know the place, he would know it when he saw it. Here he suddenly ceased to be hazy, and became alarmingly minute. He gave a description of the house detailed enough for an auctioneer. I have forgotten nearly all the details except the last two, which were that the lamp-post was painted green, and that there was a red pillar-box at the corner.

" 'A red pillar-box P I cried in astonishment. 'Why, the place must be in England P

" 'I had forgotten/ he said, nodding heavily. 'That is the island's name.'

" 'But, nom du nom/ I cried testily, 'you've just come from England, my boy.'

" 'They said it was England/ said my imbecile conspiratorily. 'They said it was Kent. But those Kentish men are such liars one can't believe anything they say.'

" 'Monsieur/ I said, 'you must pardon me. I am elderly, and the fumisteries of the young men are beyond me. I go by common sense or, at* the largest, by that extension of applied common sense called science/

" 'Science!' cried the stranger, 'there is only one good thing science ever discovered. A good thing—good tidings of great joy. That the world is round.'

"I told him with civility that his words conveyed no impression to my intelligence. 'I mean/ he said, 'that going right round the world is the shortest way to where you are already.'

" 'Is it not even shorter,' I asked, 'to stop where you are?'

" 'No, no, no,' he cried emphatically. 'That way is very long and very weary. At the end of the world, at the back of the dawn, I shall find the wife I really married, and the house that is really mine. And that house will have a greener lamp-post and a redder pillar-box. Do you,' he asked with a sudden intensity, 'do you never want to rush out of your house in order to find it.'

" 'No, I think not,' I replied, 'reason tells a man from the first to adapt his desires to the probable supply of life. I remain here content to fulfil the life of man. All my interests are here, and most of my friends, and—'

14 'And yet/ he cried, starting to his almost terrific height, 'you made the French Revolution P

11 'Pardon me,' I said, 'I am not quite so elderly. A relative perhaps.'

" 'I mean your sort did,' exclaimed this personage. 'Yes, your damned smug, settled, sensible sort made the French Revolution. Oh! I know, some say it was no good, and you're just back where you were before. Why, blast it all, that's just where we all want to be—back where we were before! That is revolution—going right round every revolution—like every repentance—is a return.'

"He was so excited that I waited till he had taken his seat again, and then said something indifferent and soothing, but he struck the tiny table with his colossal fist and went on.

" 'I am going to have a revolution, not a French Revolution, but an English Revolution. God has given to each tribe its own type of mutiny. The Frenchmen march against the citadel of the city together; the Englishman marches to the outskirts of the city, and alone. But I am going to turn the world upside down, too. I'm going to turn myself upside down. I'm going to walk upside down in the cursed upsidedownland of the Antipodes, where trees and men hang head downward in the sky. But my revolution, like yours, like the earth's, will end up in the holy, happy place, the celestial, incredible place—the place where we were before.'

"With these remarks, which can scarcely be reconciled with reason, he leapt from the seat and strode away into the twilight, swinging his pole and leaving behind him an excessive payment, which also pointed to some loss of mental balance. This is all I know of the episode of the man landed from the fishing-boat, and I hope it may serve the interests of justice.—Accept, sir, the assurances of the very high consideration, with which I have the honour to be your obedient servant,

"Jules Dudobin."

"The next document in our dossier," continued Inglewood, "comes from the town of Crazok, in the central plains of Russia, and runs as follows,—

" 'SIR,—My name is Paul Nickolaovitch: I am the station-master at the station near Crazok. The great trains go by across the plains taking people to China, but very few people get down at the platform where I have to watch. This makes my life rather lonely, and I am thrown back much upon the books I have. But I cannot discuss these very much with my neighbours, for enlightened ideas have not spread in this part of Russia so much as in other parts. Many of the peasants round here have never heard of Bernard Shaw.

" 'I am a Liberal, and do my best to spread Liberal ideas; but since the failure of the revolution this has been even more difficult. The revolutionists committed many acts contrary to the pure principles of humanitarian-ism, with which indeed, owing to the scarcity of books, they were ill acquainted. I did not approve of these cruel acts, though provoked by the badness of the government; but now there is a tendency to reproach all intelligents with the memory of them. This is very unfortunate for intelligents.

11 'It was when the railway strike was almost over, and a few trains came through at long intervals, that I stood one day watching a train that had come in. Only one person got out of the train, far away up at the other end of it; for it was a very long train. It was evening, with a cold greenish sky; a little snow had fallen, but not enough to whiten the plain, which stretched away a sort of sad purple in all directions, save where the flat tops of some distant tablelands caught the evening light like lakes. As the solitary man came stamping along on the thin snow by the train, he grew larger and larger; I thought I had never seen so large a man. But he looked even taller than he was, I think, because his shoulders were very big, and his head comparatively little. From the big shoulders hung a tattered old jacket, striped dull red and dirty white, very thin for the winter, and one hand rested on a huge pole, such as peasants rake in weeds with to burn them. " 'Before he had traversed the full length of the train he was entangled in one of those knots of rowdies that were the embers of the extinct revolution, though they mostly disgraced themselves upon the government side. I was just moving to his assistance, when he whirled up his rake and laid out to left and right with such energy that he came through them without scathe and strode right up to me, leaving them staggered and really astonished.

" 'Yet when he reached me, after so abrupt an assertion of his aim, he could only say rather dubiously in French, that he wanted a house.

" ' "There are not many houses to be had round here," I answered in the same language, "the district has been very disturbed. A revolution, as you know, has recently been suppressed. Any further building—"

" ' "Oh! I don't mean that," he cried, "I mean a real house. A live house. It really is a live house; for it runs away from me."

" *I am ashamed to say that something in his phrase or gesture moved me profoundly. We Russians are brought up in an atmosphere of folk-lore, and its unfortunate effects can still be seen in the bright colours of the children's dolls and of the ikons. For an instant the idea of a house running away from a man gave me pleasure; for the enlightenment of man moves slowly.

11 * "Have you no other house of youi own?" I asked.

" ' "I have left it," he said very sadly. "It was not the house that grew dull, but I that grew dull in it. My wife was better than all women, and yet I could not feel it."

11 * "And so," I said with sympathy, "you walked straight out of the front door, like a masculine Nora."

"""Nora?" he inquired politely, apparently supposing it to be a Russian word.

" ■ "I mean Nora in The Doll's House/ " I replied.

" 'At this he looked very much astonished, and I knew he was an Englishman; for Englishmen always think that Russians study nothing but "ukases."

" ■ " The Doll's House!' " he cried vehemently, "why, that is just where Ibsen was so wrong! Why, the whole aim of a house is to be a doll's house. Don't you remember, when you were a child, how those little windows were windows, while the big windows weren't? A child has a doll's house, and shrieks when a front door opens inwards. A banker has a real house, yet how numerous 250

are the bankers who fail to emit the faintest shriek when their real front doors open inwards."

" 'Something from the folk-lore of my infancy still kept me foolishly silent; and before I could speak, the Englishman had leaned over and was saying in a sort of loud whisper, "I have found out how to make a big thing small. I have found out how to turn a house into a doll's house. Get a long way off it. God lets us turn all things into toys by his great gift of distance. Once let me see my old brick house standing up quite little against the horizon, and I shall want to go back to it again. I shall see the funny little toy lamppost painted green outside the gate; and all the dear little people like dolls looking out of the window. For the windows really open in my doll's house."

"' "But why?" I asked, "should you wish to return to that particular doll's house? Having taken, like Nora, the bold step against convention, having made yourself in the conventional sense disreputable, having dared to be free, why should you not take advantage of your freedom? As the greatest 251

modern writers have pointed out, what you called your marriage was only your mood. You have a right to leave it all behind, like the clippings of your hair, or the parings of your nails. Having once escaped, you have the world before you. Though the words may seem strange to you, you are free in Russia."

" 'He sat with his dreamy eyes on the dark circles of the plains, where the only moving thing was the long and labouring trail of smoke out of the railway engine, violet in tint, volcanic in outline, the one hot and heavy cloud of that cold clear evening of pale green.

" c "Yes," he said with a huge sigh, "I am free in Russia, you are right. I could really walk into that town over there and have love all over again, and perhaps marry some beautiful woman and begin again, and nobody could even find me. Yes, you have certainly convinced me of something."

" 'His tone was so queer and mystical that I felt impelled to ask him what he meant, and of what exactly I had convinced him.

" ' "You have convinced me," he said, with the same dreamy eye, "why it is really wicked and dangerous for a man to run away from his wife."

"' "And why is it dangerous?" I inquired.

" ' "Why, because nobody can find him," answered this odd person, "and we all want to be found."

"' "The most original modern thinkers," I remarked, "Ibsen, Gorki, Nietzsche, Shaw, would all say rather that what we want most is to be lost. To find ourselves in untrodden paths, and to do unprecedented things; to break with the past and belong to the future."

" 'He rose to his whole height somewhat sleepily, and looked round on what was, I confess, a somewhat desolate scene; the dark purple plains, the neglected railroad, the few ragged knots of the malcontents. "I shall not find the house here," he said. "It is still eastward—further and further eastward."

" 'Then he turned upon me with something like fury, and struck the foot of his pole upon the frozen earth.

"' "And if I do go back to my country," he cried, "I may be locked up in a madhouse before I reach my own house. I have been a bit unconventional in my time! Why, Nietzsche stood in a row of ramrods in the silly old Prussian army, and Shaw takes temperance beverages in the suburbs; but the things I do are unprecedented things. This round road I am treading is an untrodden path. I do believe in breaking out; I am a revolutionist. But don't you see that all these real leaps and destructions and escapes are only attempts to get back to Eden—to something we have had, to something at least we have heard of? Don't you see one only breaks the fence or shoots the moon in order to get home?"

u i «N 0 » i answered after due reflection. "I don't think I should accept that."

" ' "Ah," he said with a sort of sigh, "then you have explained a second thing to me."

"""What do you mean?" I asked; "what thing?"

"' "Why, your revolution has failed," he said, and walking across quite suddenly to the train he got into it just as it was steaming. Away at last; and I saw the long snaky tail of it disappear along the darkening flats.

" 'I saw no more of him; but though his views were adverse to the best advanced thought, he struck me as an interesting person. I should like to find out if he has produced any literary works.—Yours, etc.,

" 'Paul Nickolaovitch,' "

There was something in this odd set of glimpses into foreign lives which kept the absurd tribunal quieter than it had hitherto been, and it was again without interruption that Inglewood opened another paper upon his pile. "The Court will be indulgent," he said, "if the next note lacks the special ceremonies of our letter-writing. It is ceremonious enough in its own way."

"The Celestial Principles are permanent: greeting.—I am Wong-Hi, and I tend the temple of all the ancestors of my family in the forest of Fu. The man that broke through the sky and came to me said that it must be very dull, but I showed him the wrongness of his thought. I am indeed in one place, for my uncle took me to this temple when I was a boy, and in this I shall doubtless die. But if a man remain in one place he shall see that the place changes. The pagoda of my temple stands up silently out of all the trees, like a yellow pagoda above many green pagodas. But the skies are sometimes blue like porcelain, and sometimes green like jade, and sometimes red like garnet. But the night is always ebony, and always returns, said the Emperor Ho.

" 'The sky-breaker came at evening very suddenly, for I had hardly seen any stirring in the tops of the green trees over which I look as over a sea, when I go to the top of the temple at morning. And yet when he came, it was as if an elephant had strayed from the armies of the great kings of India. For palms snapped, and bamboos broke, and there came forth in the sunshine before the temple one taller than the sons of men.

" 'Strips of red and white hung about him like ribbons of a carnival, and he carried a pole with a row of teeth on it like the teeth of a dragon. His face was white and discomposed after the fashion of the foreigners, so that they look like dead men, filled with devils; and he spoke our speech brokenly.

" 'He said to me, "This is only a temple, I am trying to find a house." And then he told me with indelicate haste that the lamp outside his home was green, and that there was a red post at the corner of it.

" ' "I have not seen your house or any houses," I answered. "I dwell in this temple and serve the gods."

" ' "Do you believe in the gods?" he asked with hunger in his eyes, like the hunger of dogs. And this seemed to me a strange question to ask, for what should a man do except what men have done?

" ' ■ "My lord," I said, "it must be good for men to hold up their hands even if the skies are empty. For if there are gods, they will be pleased, and if there are none, then there are none to be displeased. Sometimes the skies are gold and sometimes porphyry and sometimes ebony, but the trees and the temple stand still under all. So the great Confucius taught us that if we do always the same things with our hands and our feet as do the wise beasts and birds, with our heads we may think many things; yes, my lord, and doubt many things. So long as men offer rice at the right season, and kindle lanterns at the right hour, it matters little whether there be gods or no. For these things are not to appease gods, but to appease men."

" 'He came yet closer to me, so that he seemed enormous; yet his look was very gentle.

" ' "Break your temple," he said, "and your gods will be freed."

" 'And I, smiling at his simplicity, answered : "And so, if there be no gods, I shall have nothing but a broken temple."

" 'And at this, that giant from whom the light of reason was withheld threw out his mighty arms and asked me to forgive him. And when I asked him for what he should be forgiven he answered: "For being right."

" ' "Your idols and emperors are so old and wise and satisfying," he cried; "it is a shame that they should be wrong. We are so vulgar and violent; we have done you so many iniquities—it is a shame that we should be right after all."

" 'And I, still enduring his harmlessness, asked him why he thought that he and his people were right.

" 'And he answered, "We are right because we are bound where men should be bound, and free where men should be free. We are right because we doubt and destroy laws and customs—but we do not doubt our own right to destroy them. For you live by customs, but we by creeds. Behold me—in my country I am called Smith. My country is abandoned, my name is defiled, because I pursue across the world what really belongs to me. You are steadfast as the trees, because you do not believe. I am as fickle as the tempest because I do believe. I do believe in my own house, which I shall find again. And at the last remaineth the green lantern and the red post."

" 'I said to him, "At the last remaineth only wisdom."

" 'But even as I said the word he uttered a horrible shout, and rushing forward disappeared among the trees. I have not seen this man again nor any other man. The virtues of the wise are of fine brass.

" <WONG-HI.'"

"The next letter I have to read," proceeded Arthur Inglewood, "will probably make clear the nature of our client's curious but innocent experiment. It is dated from a mountain village in California, and runs as follows,—

" \'7b SIR,—A person answering to the rather extraordinary description required certainly went, some time ago, over the high pass of the Sierras, on which I live and of which I am probably the sole stationary inhabitant. I keep a rudimentary tavern, rather ruder than a hut, on the very top of this specially steep and threatening pass. My name is Louis Hara, and the very name may puzzle you about my nationality. Well, it puzzles me a great deal. When one has been for fifteen years without society it is hard to have patriotism; and where there is not even a hamlet it is difficult to invent a nation. My father was an Irishman of the fiercest and most free-shooting of the old California kind. My mother was a Spaniard, proud of descent from the old Spanish families round San Francisco, yet accused for all that of some admixture of Red Indian blood. I was well educated and fond of music and books. But like many other hybrids, I was too bad or too good for the world; and after attempting many things, I was glad enough to get a sufficient though a lonely living in this little carabet in the mountains. In my solitude I fell into many of the ways of a savage. Like an Eskimo I was shapeless in winter. Like a Red Indian, I wore in hot summers nothing but a pair of leather trousers, with a great straw hat as big as a parasol to defend me from the sun. I had a bowie knife at my belt and a long gun under my arm; and I dare say I produced a pretty wild impression on the few peaceable travellers that could climb up to my place. But I promise you I never looked as mad as that man did. Compared to him I was Fifth Avenue.

" 'I dare say that living under the very tops of the Sierras has an odd effect on the mind; one tends to think of those last lonely rocks not as peaks coming to a point, but rather as pillars holding up heaven itself. Straight cliffs sail up and away beyond the hope of the eagles; cliffs so tall that they seem to attract the stars and collect them as sea-crags collect a mere glitter of phosphorous. These terraces and towers of rock do not, like smaller crests, seem to be the end of the world. Rather they seem to be its awful beginning: its huge foundations. We could almost fancy the mountain branching out above us like a tree of stone, and carrying all those cosmic lights like a candelabrum. For just as the peaks failed us, soaring impossibly far, so the stars crowded us (as it seemed), coming impossibly near. The spheres burst about us more like thunderbolts hurled at the earth than planets circling placidly about it.

" 'All this may have driven me mad: I am not sure. I know there is one angle of the road down the pass where the rock leans out a little; and on windy nights I seem to hear it clashing overhead with other rocks— yes, city against city and citadel against citadel, far up into the night. It was on such an evening that the strange man struggled up the pass. Broadly speaking, only strange men did struggle up the pass. But I had never seen one like this one before.

" 'He carried (I cannot conceive why) a long, dilapidated garden rake, all bearded and bedraggled with grasses, so that it looked like the ensign of some old barbarian tribe. His hair, which was as long and rank as the grass, hung down below his huge shoulders; and such clothes as clung about him were rags and tongues of red and yellow, so that he had the air of being dressed like an Indian in feathers or autumn leaves. The rake or pitchfork, or whatever it was, he used sometimes as an alpenstock, sometimes (I was told) as a weapon. I do not know why he should have used it as a weapon, for he had, and afterwards showed me, an excellent six-shooter in his pocket. "But that," he said, "I use only for peaceful purposes." I have no notion what he meant.

11 'He sat down on the rough bench outside my inn and drank some wine from the vineyards below; sighing with ecstasy over it like one who had travelled long among alien cruel things and found at last something that he knew. Then he sat staring rather foolishly at the rude lantern of lead and coloured glass that hangs over my door. It is old but of no value, my grandmother gave it me long ago: she was devout, and it happens that the glass is painted with a crude picture of Bethlehem and the Wise Men and the Star. He seemed so mesmerized with the transparent glow of Our Lady's blue gown and the big gold star behind, that he led me also to look at the thing, which I had not done for fourteen years.

" 'Then he slowly withdrew his eyes from this and looked out eastward where the road fell away below us. The sunset sky was a vault of rich violet, fading away into mauve and silver round the edges of the dark mountain amphitheatre, and between us and the ravine below rose up out of the deeps and went up into the heights the straight solitary rock we call Green Finger. Of a queer volcanic colour, and wrinkled all over with what looks undecipherable writing, it hung there like a Babylonian pillar or needle.

" The man silently stretched out his rake in that direction; and before he spoke I knew what he meant. Beyond the great green rock in the purple sky hung a single star.

" ' "A star in the East," he said in a strange hoarse voice like one of our ancient eagle's, "the wise men followed the star and found the house. But if I followed the star, should I find the house?"

"' "It depends perhaps," I said, smiling, "on whether you are a wise man." I refrained from adding that he certainly didn't look it.

" * "You may judge for yourself," he answered, "I am a man who left his own house because he could no longer bear to be away from it."

" ■ "It certainly sounds paradoxical," I said.

" ' "I heard my wife and children talking and saw them moving about the room," he continued, "and all the time I knew they were walking and talking in another house thousands of miles away, under the light of different skies, and beyond the series of the seas. I loved them with a devouring love, because they seemed not only distant but unattainable. Never did human creatures seem so dear and so desirable: but I seemed like a cold ghost. I loved them intolerably; therefore, I cast off their dust from my feet for a testimony. Nay, I did more. I spurned the world under my feet so that it swung full circle like a treadmill."

" ( "Do you really mean," I cried, "that you have come right round the world? Your speech is English, yet you are coming from the west."

" ' "My pilgrimage is not yet accomplished," he replied sadly; "I have become a pilgrim to cure myself of being an exile."

" 'Something in the word "pilgrim" awoke down in the roots of my ruinous experience, memories of what my fathers had felt about the world, and of something from whence I came. I looked again at the little pictured lantern at which I had not looked for fourteen years.

" ' "My grandmother," I said in a low tone, "would have said that we were all in exile, and that no earthly house could cure the holy homesickness that forbids us rest."

" 'He was silent a long while, and watched a single eagle drift out beyond the Green Finger into the darkening void.

" Then he said, "I think your grandmother was right," and stood up leaning on his grassy pole. "I think that must be the reason," he said, "the secret of this life of man, so ecstatic and so unappeased. But I think there is more to be said. I think God has given us the love of special places, of a hearth and of a native land, for a good reason."

"' "I dare say," I said, "what reason!"

" l "Because otherwise," he said, pointing his pole out at the sky and the abyss, "we might worship that."

<< i

"What do you mean?" I demanded.

ut "Eternity," he said in his harsh voice, "the largest of the idols—the mightiest of the rivals of God."

" ' "You mean pantheism and infinity and all that," I suggested.

" ' "I mean," he said with increasing vehemence, "that if there be a house for me in heaven it will either have a green lamp-post and a hedge, or something quite as positive and personal as a green lamp-post and a hedge. I mean that God bade me love one spot and serve it, and do all things however wild in praise of it, so that this one spot might be a witness against all the infinities and the sophistries, that Paradise is somewhere and not anywhere, is something and not anything. And I would not be so very much surprised if the house in heaven had a real green lamp-post after all."

" 'With which he shouldered his pole and went striding down the perilous paths below, and left me alone with the eagles. But since he went a fever of homelessness will often shake me. I am troubled by rainy meadows and mud cabins I have never seen; and I wonder whether America will endure.—Yours faithfully,

" 'Louis Hara.' "

After a short silence Inglewood said: "And finally, we desire to put in as evidence the following document,—

" 'This is to say that I am Ruth Davis, and have been housemaid to Mrs. I. Smith at "The Laurels" in Croydon for the last six months. When I came the lady was alone with two children; she was not a widow, but her husband was away. She was left with plenty of money and did not seem disturbed about him, though she often hoped he would be back soon. She said he was rather eccentric and a little change did him good. One evening last week I was bringing the tea-things out on to the lawn when I nearly dropped them. The end of a long rake was suddenly stuck over the hedge, and planted like a jumping-pole; and over the hedge, just like a monkey on a stick, came a huge horrible man, all hairy and ragged like Robinson Crusoe. I screamed out, but my mistress didn't even get out of her chair; but smiled and said he wanted shaving. Then he sat down quite calmly at the garden table and took a cup of tea, and then I realized that this must be Mr. Smith himself. He has stopped here ever since and does not really give much trouble, though I sometimes fancy he is a little weak in his head.

"'Ruth Davis. " 'P.S. —I forgot to say that he looked round at the garden and said, very loud and strong, "Oh, what a lovely place you've got;" just as if he'd never seen it before.' "

The room had been growing dark and drowsy; the afternoon sun sent one heavy shaft of powdered gold across it, which fell with an intangible solemnity upon the empty seat of Mary Gray; for the younger women had left the court before the more recent of the investigations. Mrs. Duke was still asleep, and Innocent Smith, looking like a huge hunchback in the twilight, was bending closer and closer to his paper toys. But the five men really engaged in the controversy, and concerned not to convince the tribunal but to convince each other, still sat round the table like the Committee of Public Safety.

Suddenly Moses Gould banged one big scientific book on top of another, cocked his little legs up against the table, tipped his chair backwards so far as to be in direct danger of falling over, emitted a startling and prolonged whistle like a steam engine, and asserted that it was all his eye.

When asked by Moon what was all his eye, he banged down behind the books again and answered with considerable excitement, throwing his papers about, "All those fairy-tales you've been reading out," he said. "Oh! don't talk to me 1 I ain't littery and that, but I know fairy-tales when I hear 'em. I got a bit stumped in some of the philosophical bits and felt inclined to go out for a B and S. But we're living in West 'Ampstead and not in 'Ell; and the long and the short of it is that some things 'appen and some things don't 'appen. Those are the things that don't 'appen."

"I thought," said Moon gravely, "that we quite clearly explained—"

"Oh, yes, old chap, you quite clearly explained," assented Mr. Gould, with extraordinary volubility; "you'd explain an elephant off the doorstep, you would. I ain't a clever chap like you; but I ain't a born natural, Michael Moon, and when there's an elephant on my doorstep I don't listen to no explanations. 'It's got a trunk,' I says.—'My trunk,' you says. 'I'm fond of travellin' and a change does me good.'—'But the blasted thing's got tusks,' I says.—'Don't look a gift 'orse in the mouth,' you says, 'but thank the goodness and the graice that on your birth 'as smiled.'— 'But it's nearly as big as the 'ouse,' I says.— 'That's the bloomin' perspective,' you says, 'and the saicred magic of distance.'—'Why, the elephant's trumpetin' like the Day of Judgment,' I says.—'That's your own conscience a' talkin' to you, Moses Gould,' you says in a grive and tender voice.—'Well, I 'ave got a conscience as much as you; I don't believe most of the things they tell you in church on Sundays; and I don't believe these 'ere things any more because you goes on about 'em as if you was in church. I believe an elephant's a great big, ugly, dingerous beast— and I believe Smith's another."

"Do you mean to say," asked Inglewood, "that you still doubt the evidence of exculpation we have brought forward?"

"Yes, I do still doubt it," said Gould warmly. "It's all a bit too far-fetched, and some of it a bit too far off. 'Ow can we test all those tales? 'Ow can we drop in and buy the 'Pink 'Un' at the railway station at Kosky Wosky or whatever it was? 'Ow can we go and do a gargle at that saloon-bar on top of the Sierra Mountains? But anybody can go and see Bunting's boarding-house at Worth-ing."

Moon regarded him with an expression of real or assumed surprise.

"Any one," continued Gould, "can call on Mr. Trip."

"It is a comforting thought," replied Michael, with restraint, "but why should any one call on Mr. Trip?"

"For just exactly the sime reason," cried the excited Moses, hammering on the table with both hands, "for just exactly the sime reason that he should communicate with Messrs. 'Anbury and Bootle of Paternoster Row and with Miss Gridley's 'igh class Academy at 'Endin, and with old Lady Bullingdon who lives at Penge."

"Again, to go at once to the moral roots of life," said Michael, "why is it among the duties of man to communicate with old Lady Bullingdon who lives at Penge?"

"It ain't one of the duties of man," said Gould, "nor one of his pleasures either, I can tell you. She takes the crumpet, does Lady Bullingdon at Penge. But it's one of the duties of a prosecutor pursuin' the innocent, blameless butterfly career of your friend Smith, and it's the sime with all the others I mentioned."

"But why do you bring in these people here?" asked Inglewood.

"Why, because we've got proof enough to sink a steamboat," roared Moses. "Because I've got the papers in my very 'and, because your precious Innocent is a blackguard and 'ome smasher, and these are the 'omes he's smashed. I don't set up for an 'oly man; but I wouldn't 'ave all those poor girls on my conscience for something. And I think a chap that's capable of desertin' and perhaps killin'

'em all, is about capable of crackin' a crib or it shootin' an old schoolmaster—so I don't care much about the other yarns one way or another."

"I think," said Dr. Cyrus Pym, with a refined cough, "that we are approaching this matter rather irregularly. This is really the fourth charge on the charge sheet, and perhaps I had better put it before you in an ordered and scientific manner."

Nothing but a fainf groan from Michael broke the silence of the darkening room.

## CHAPTER IV

### THE WILD WEDDINGS; OR, THE POLYGAMY CHARGE

it A MODERN man," said Dr. Cyrus l\ Pym, "must—if he be thoughtful— approach the problem of marriage with some caution. Marriage is a stage—doubtless a suitable stage—in the long advance of mankind towards a goal which we cannot as yet conceive; which we are not, perhaps, yet fitted even to desire. What, gentlemen, is now the ethical position of marriage? Have we outlived it?"

"Outlived it?" broke out Moon. "Why, nobody's even survived it! Look at all the people married since Adam and Eve—and all as dead as mutton."

"This is no doubt an interpellation joc'lar in its character," said Dr. Pym frigidly. "I cannot tell what may be Mr. Moon's matured and ethical view of marriage—"

"I can tell," said Michael savagely, out of the gloom; "marriage is a duel to the death which no man of honour should decline."

"Michael," said Arthur Inglewood in a low voice, "you must keep quiet."

"Mr. Moon," said Pym with exquisite good temper, "probably regards the institution in a more antiquated manner. Probably he would make it stringent and uniform. He would treat divorce in some great soul of steel—the divorce of a Julius Caesar or of a Salt-king Robinson— exactly as he would treat some no-account tramp or labourer who scoots from his wife. Science has views broader and more humane. Just as murder for the scientist is a thirst for absolute destruction, just as theft for the scientist is a hunger for monotonous acquisition, so polygamy for the scientist is an extreme development of the instinct for variety. A man thus afflicted is incapable of constancy. Doubtless there is a physical cause for this flitting from flower to flower—as there is doubtless for the intermittent groaning which appears to afflict Mr. Moon at the present moment. Our own world-scorning Winterbottom has even dared to say, 'For a certain rare and fine physical type free polygamy is but the realization of the variety of females, as comradeship is the realization of the variety of males.' In any case, the type that tends to variety is recognized by all authoritative inquirers. Such a type, if the widower of a negress, does in many ascertained cases espouse en seconde noces an albino; such a type, when freed from the gigantic embraces of a female Patagonian, will often evolve from its own imaginative instinct the consoling figure of an Eskimo. To such a type there can be no doubt that the prisoner belongs. If blind doom and unbearable temptation constitute any slight excuse for a man, there is no doubt that he has these excuses.

"Earlier in the inquiry, the defence showed real chivalric ideality in admitting half of our story wthout further dispute. We should like to acknowledge and imitate so eminently large-hearted a style by conceding also that the story told by Curate Percy about the canoe, the weir, and the young wife seems to be substantially true. Apparently Smith did marry a young woman he had nearly run down in a boat; it only remains to be considered whether it would not have been kinder of him to have murdered her instead of marrying her. In confirmation of this fact I can now concede to the defence an unquestionable record of such a marriage."

So saying, he handed across to Michael a cutting from the Maidenhead Gazette, which distinctly recorded the marriage of the daughter of a "coach," a tutor well known in the place, to Mr. Innocent Smith, late of Brake-speare College, Cambridge.

When Dr. Pym resumed it was realized that his face had grown at once both tragic and triumphant.

"I pause upon this preliminary fact," he said seriously, "because this fact alone would give us the victory, were we aspiring after victory and not after truth. As far as the personal and domestic problem holds us, that problem is solved. Dr. Warner and I entered this house at an instant of highly emotional diff'culty. England's Warner has entered many houses to save human kind from sickness—this time he entered to save an innocent lady from a walking pestilence. Smith was just about to carry away a young girl from this house; his cab and bag were at the very door. He had told her she was going to await the marriage licence at the house of his aunt. That aunt," continued Cyrus Pym, his face darkening grandly, "—that visionary aunt had been the dancing will-o'-the-wisp who had led many a high-souled maiden to her doom. Into how many virginal ears has he whispered that holy word? When he said 'aunt' there glowed about her all the merriment and high morality of the Anglo-Saxon home. Kettles began to hum, pussy cats to purr, in that very wild cab that was being driven to destruction."

Inglewood looked up, to find, to his astonishment (as many another denizen of the eastern hemisphere has found), that the American was not only perfectly serious, but was really eloquent and affecting—when the difference of the hemispheres was adjusted.

"It is, therefore, atrociously evident that the man Smith has at least represented himself to one innocent female of this house as an eligible bachelor, being in fact a married man. I agree with my colleague, Mr. Gould, that no other crime could approximate to this. As to whether what our ancestors called purity has any ultimate ethical value indeed, science hesitates with a high, proud hesitation. But what hesitation can there be about the baseness of a citizen who ventures, by brutal experiments upon living females, to anticipate the verdict of science on such a point?"

"The woman mentioned by Curate Percy as living with Smith in Highbury, may or may not be the same as the lady he married in Maidenhead. If one short sweet spell of constancy and heart repose interrupted the plunging torrent of his profligate life, we will not deprive him of that long past possibility. After that conjectural date, alas, he seems to have plunged deeper and deeper into the shaking quagmires of infidelity and shame."

Dr. Pym closed his eyes: but the unfortunate fact that there was no more light left this familiar signal without its full and proper moral effect. After a pause, which almost partook of the character of prayer, he continued,—

"The first instance of the accused's repeated and irregular nuptials," he exclaimed, "comes from Lady Bullingdon; who expresses herself with the high haughtiness which must be excused in those who look out upon all mankind from the turrets of a Norman and ancestral keep. The communication she has sent to us runs as follows,—

" 'Lady Bullingdon recalls the painful incident to which reference is made, and has no desire to deal with it in detail. The girl, Polly Green, was a perfectly adequate dressmaker, and lived in the village for about two years. Her unattached condition was bad for her as well as for the general morality of the village. Lady Bullingdon, therefore, allowed it to be understood that she favoured the marriage of the young woman. The villagers naturally wishing to oblige Lady Bullingdon, came forward in several cases; and all would have been well had it not Deen for the deplorable eccentricity or depravity of the girl Green herself. Lady Bullingdon supposes that where there is a village there must be a village idiot; and in her village, it seems, there was one of these wretched creatures. Lady Bullingdon only saw him once; and she is quite aware that it is really difficult to distinguish between actual idiots and the ordinary heavy type of the rural lower classes. She noticed, however, the startling smallness of his head in comparison to the rest of his body; and, indeed, the fact of his having appeared upon election day wearing the rosette of both the two opposing parties appears to Lady Bul-lingdon to put the matter beyond a doubt. Lady Bullingdon was astounded to learn that this afflicted being had put himself forward as one of the suitors of the girl in question. Lady Bullingdon's nephew interviewed the wretch upon the point, telling him that he was a donkey to dream of such a thing, and actually received, along with an imbecile grin, the answer that donkeys generally go after carrots. But Lady Bullingdon was yet further amazed to find the unhappy girl inclined to accept this monstrous proposal; though she was actually asked in marriage by Garth, the undertaker, a man in a far superior position to her own. Lady Bullingdon could not, of course, countenance such an arrangement for a moment, and the two unhappy persons escaped for a clandestine marriage. Lady Bullingdon cannot exactly recall the man's name, but thinks it was Smith. He was always called in the village the Innocent. Later, Lady Bullingdon believes he murdered Green in a mental outbreak.'

"The next communication," proceeded Pym, "is more conspicuous for brevity, but I am of opinion that it will adequately convey its upshot. It is dated from the offices of Messrs. Hanbury and Bootle, publishers, and is as follows,—

" 'Sir, —Yrs red and conts noted. Rumour re typewriter possibly refers to a Miss Blake or similar name, feft here nine years ago to marry an organ-grinder. Case was undoubtedly curious and attracted police attention. Girl worked excellently till about Oct. 1907, when apparently went mad. Record was written at the time, part of which I enclose.—Yrs., etc., u < w TRIp ,

"The fuller statement runs as follows:—

" 'On October 12 a letter was sent from this office to Messrs. Bernard and Juke, bookbinders. Opened by Mr. Juke it was found to contain the following, "Sir, our Mr. Trip will call at 3 as we wish to know whether it is really decided 0000007366 I Ml! xy." To this Mr. Juke, a person of playful mind, returned the answer. "Sir, after consulting all the members of the firm, I am in a position to give it as my most decided opinion that it is not really decided that 0000007366 !!!!! xy. — Yrs., etc.,

11 < "J. Juke."

" ( On receiving this extraordinary reply, our Mr. Trip asked for the original letter sent from him, and found that the typewriter had indeed substituted these demented hieroglyphics for the sentences really dictated to her. Our Mr. Trip interviewed the girl; fearing that she was in an unbalanced state, and was not much reassured when she merely remarked that she always went like that when she heard the barrel-organ. Becoming yet more hysterical and extravagant, she made a series of most improbable statements, as that she was engaged to the barrel-organ man, that he was in the habit of serenading her on that instrument, that she was in the habit of playing back to him upon the typewriter (in the style of King Richard and Blondel), and that the organ man's musical ear was so exquisite and his adoration of herself so ardent that he could detect the note of the different letters on the machine, and was enraptured by them as by a melody. To all these statements of course our Mr. Trip and the rest of us only paid that sort of assent that is paid to persons who must as quickly as possible be put in the charge of their relations. But on our conducting the lady downstairs, her story received the most startling and even exasperating confirmation; for the organ-grinder, an enormous man with a small head and manifestly a fellow-lunatic, had pushed his barrel-organ in at the office doors like a battering-ram, and was boisterously demanding his alleged fiancee. When I myself came on the scene he was flinging his great, ape-like arms about and reciting a poem to her. But we were used to lunatics coming and reciting poems in our office, and we were not quite prepared for what followed. The actual verse he uttered began, I think,

"A vivid, inviolate head Ringed—"

but he never got any further. Mr. Trip made a sharp movement towards him, and the next moment the giant picked up the poor lady typewriter like a doll, sat her on top of the organ, ran it with a crash out of the office doors and raced away down the street like a flying wheelbarrow. Fve put the police upon the matter; but no trace of the amazing pair could ever be found. I was sorry myself; for the lady was not only pleasant but unusually cultivated for her position. As I am leaving the service of Messrs. Hanbury and Bootle, I put these things in a record and leave it with them. Ui (Signed) Aubrey Clarke,

"'Publishers' Reader/'"

"And the last document," said Dr. Pym complacently, "is from one of those high-souled women who have in this age introduced your English girlhood to hockey, the higher mathematics, and every form of ideality.

" 'DEAR Sir' (she writes),—'I have no objection to telling you the facts about the absurd incident you mention, though I would ask you to communicate them with some caution, for such things, however entertaining in the abstract, are not always auxiliary to the success of a girls' school. The truth is this: I wanted some one to deliver a lecture on a philological or historical question, a lecture which, while containing solid educational matter, should be a little more popular and entertaining than usual, as it was the last lecture of the term. I remembered that a Mr. Smith, of Cambridge, had written somewhere or other an amazing essay about his own somewhat ubiquitous name, an essay which showed considerable real knowledge of genealogy and topography. I wrote to him, asking if he would come and give us a bright address upon English surnames, and he did. It was very bright, almost too bright. To put the matter otherwise, by the time that he was half-way through it became apparent to the other mistresses and myself that the man was totally and entirely off his head. He began rationally enough by dealing with the two departments of place names and trade names, and he said (quite rightly, I dare say) that the loss of all significance in names was an instance of the deadening of civilization. But he then went on calmly to maintain that every man who had a place name ought to go to live in that place, and that every man who had a trade name ought instantly to adopt that trade; that people named after colours should always dress in those colours, and that people named after trees or plants (such as Beech or Rose) ought to surround and decorate themselves with these vegetables. In a slight discussion that arose afterwards among the elder girls, the difficulties of the proposal were clearly, and even eagerly, pointed out. It was urged, for instance, by Miss Younghusband that it was substantially impossible for her to play the part assigned to her; Miss Mann was in a similar dilemma, from which no modern views on the sexes could apparently extricate her; and some young ladies, whose surnames happened to be Low, Coward, and Craven, were quite enthusiastic against the idea. But all this happened afterwards. What happened at the crucial moment was that the lecturer produced several horseshoes and a large iron hammer from his bag, announced his immediate intention of setting up a smithy in the neighbourhood, and called on every one to rise in the same cause as for a heroic revolution. The other mistresses and I attempted to stop the wretched man, but I must confess that by an accident this very intercession produced the worst explosion of his insanity. He was waving the hammer, and wildly demanding the names of everybody; and it so happened that Miss Brown, one of the girls, was wearing a brown dress—a reddish-brown dress that went quietly enough with the warmer colour of her hair, as well she knew. She was a nice girl, and nice girls do know about those things. But when our maniac discovered that we really had a Miss Brown who was brown, his idee fixe blew up like a powder magazine, and there, in the presence of all the mistresses and girls, he publicly proposed to the lady in the red-brown dress. You can imagine the effect of such a scene at a girls' school. At least, if you fail to imagine it, I certainly fail to describe it.

" 'Of course the anarchy died down in a week or two, and I can think of it now as a joke. There was only one curious detail, which I will tell you as you say your inquiry is vital, but I should desire you to consider it a little more confidential than the rest. Miss Brown, who was an excellent girl in every way, did quite suddenly and surreptitiously leave us only a day or two afterwards. I should never have thought that her head would be the one to be really turned by so absurd an excitement.    Believe me, yours faithfully,

"'Ada Gridley.'

"I think," said Pym with a really convincing simplicity and seriousness, "that these letters speak for themselves."

Mr. Moon rose for the last time in a darkness that gave no hint of whether his native gravity was mixed with his native irony.

"Throughout this inquiry," he said, "but especially in this its closing phase, the prosecution has perpetually relied on one argument; I mean the fact that no one knows what has become of all the unhappy women apparently seduced by Smith. There is no sort of proof that they were murdered, but that implication is perpetually made when the question is asked as to how they died. Now I am not interested in how they died, or when they died, or whether they died. But I am interested in another analogous question—that of how they were born, and when they were born, and whether they were born. Do not misunderstand me. I do not dispute the existence of these women, or the veracity of those who have witnessed to them. I merely remark on the notable fact that only one of these victims, the Maidenhead girl, is described as having any home or parents. All the rest are boarders or birds of passage—a guest, a solitary dressmaker, a bachelor-girl doing typewriting. Lady Bullingdon, looking from her turrets, which she bought from the Whartons with the old soap-boiler's money when she jumped at marrying an unsuccessful gentleman from Ulster—Lady Bullingdon, looking out from those turrets, did really see an object which she describes as Green. Mr. Trip, of Han-bury & Booties, really did have a typewriter betrothed to Smith. Miss Gridley, though idealistic, is absolutely honest. She did house, feed, and teach a young woman, whom Smith succeeded in decoying away. We admit that all these women really lived. But we still ask whether they were ever born?"

"Oh, crikey," said Moses Gould, stifled with amusement.

"There could hardly," interposed Pym, with a quiet smile, "be a better instance of the neglect of true scientific processes. The scientist, when once convinced of the fact of vitality and consciousness, would infer from these the previous processes of generation."

"If these gals," said Gould impatiently—"if these gals were all alive (all alive O!) I'd chance a fiver they were all born."

"You'd lose your fiver," said Michael, speaking gravely out of the gloom. "All those admirable ladies were alive. They were more alive for having come into contact with Smith. They were all quite definitely alive, but only one of them was ever born."

"Are you asking us to believe—" began Dr. Pym.

"I am asking you a second question," said Moon sternly. "Can the court now sitting throw any light on a truly singular circumstance? Dr. Pym in his interesting lecture on what are called, I believe, the relations of the sexes, said that Smith was the slave of a lust for variety which would lead a man first to a negress and then to an albino, first to a Pata-gonian giantess and then to a tiny Eskimo. But is there any evidence of such variety here? Is there any trace of a gigantic Patagonian in the story? Was the typewriter an Eskimo? So picturesque a circumstance would not surely have escaped remark. Was Lady Bul-lingdon's dressmaker a negress? A voice in my bosom answers, 'No!' Lady Bullingdon, I am sure, would think a negress so conspicuous as to be almost socialistic, and would feel something a little rakish even about an albino. "But was there in Smith's taste any such variety as the learned doctor describes? So far as our slight materials go, the very opposite seems to be the case. We have only one actual description of any of the prisoner's wives—the short but highly poetic account by the aesthetic curate. 'Her dress was the colour of spring and her hair of autumn leaves.' Autumn leaves, of course, are of various colours, some of which would be rather startling in hair (green, for instance) ; but I think such an expression would be most naturally used of the shades from red-brown to red, especially as ladies with their coppery-coloured hair do frequently wear light artistic greens. Now when we come to the next wife, we find the eccentric lover, when told he is a donkey, answering that donkeys always go after carrots; a remark which Lady Bullingdon evidently regarded as pointless and part of the natural table-talk of a village idiot, but which has an obvious meaning if we suppose that Polly's hair was red. Passing to the next wife, the one he took from the girls' school, we find Miss Gridley noticing that the schoolgirl in question wore 'a reddish-brown dress, that went quietly enough with the warmer colour of her hair.' In other words, the colour of the girl's hair was something redder than red-brown. Lastly, the romantic organ-grinder declaimed in the office some poetry that only got as far as the words,—

'O vivid inviolate head Ringed—'

But I think a wide study of the worst modern poets will enable us to guess that 'ringed with a glory of red,' or 'ringed with its passionate red' was the line that rhymed to 'head.' In this case once more, therefore, there is good reason to suppose that Smith, free in love with a girl with some sort of auburn or darkish red hair—rather," he said, looking down at the table, "rather like Miss Gray's hair."

Cyrus Pym was leaning forward with lowered eyelids, ready with one of his more pedantic interpolations, but Moses Gould suddenly struck his forefinger on his nose, with an expression of extreme astonishment and intelligence in his brilliant eyes.

"Mr. Moon's contention at present," interposed Pym, "is not, even if veracious, inconsistent with the lunatico-criminal view of I. Smith, which we have nailed to the mast. Science has long anticipated such a complication. An incurable attraction to a particular type of physical woman is one of the commonest of criminal perversities, and when not considered narrowly, but in the light of induction and evolution—"

"At this late stage," said Michael Moon very quietly, "I may perhaps relieve myself of a simple emotion that has been pressing me throughout the proceedings, by saying that induction and evolution may go and boil themselves. The Missing Link and all that is well enough for kids—but I'm talking about things we know. All we know of the Missing Link is that he is missing—and he won't be missed either. I know all about his human head and his horrid tail—they belong to a very old game called 'Heads I win, tails you lose.' If you do find a fellow's bones, it proves he lived a long while ago; if you don't find his bones it proves how long ago he lived. That is the game you've been playing with this Smith affair. Because Smith's head is small for his shoulders you call him Microcephalous. If it had been large, you'd have called it Water-on-the-brain. As long as poor old Smith's seraglio seemed pretty various, variety was the sign of madness. Now because it's turning out to be a bit monochrome, now monotony is the sign of madness. I suffer from all the disadvantages of being a grownup person, and I'm jolly well going to get some of the advantages, too, and with all politeness I propose not to be bullied with long words instead of short reasons, or consider your business a triumphant progress merely because you're always finding out that you were wrong. Having relieved myself of these feelings, I have merely to add that I regard Dr. Pym as an ornament to the world far more beautiful than the Parthenon or the monument on Bunker's Hill, and that I propose to resume and conclude my remarks on the many marriages of Mr. Innocent Smith.

"Besides this red hair, there is another unifying thread that runs through these scattered incidents. There is something very peculiar and suggestive about the names of these women. Mr. Trip, you will remember, said he thought the typewriter's name was Blake, but could not remember exactly. I suggest that it might very well have been Black, and in that case we have a curious series: Miss Green in Lady Bullingdon's village; Miss Brown at the Hendon School; Miss Black at the publishers. A choice of colour as it were; which ends up with Miss Gray at Beacon House, West Hampstead."

Amid a dead silence Moon continued his exposition. "What is the meaning of this queer coincidence about colours? Personally I cannot doubt for a moment that these names are purely arbitrary names, assumed as part of some general scheme or joke. I think it very probable that they were taken from a series of costumes—that Polly Green only meant Polly (or Mary) when in green, and that Mary Gray only means Mary (or Polly) when in gray. This would explain—"

Cyrus Pym was standing up rigid and almost pallid. "Do you actually mean to suggest—" he cried.

"Yes," said Michael. "I do mean to suggest that. Innocent Smith has had many woo-ngs and many weddings, for all I know; but he has had only one wife. She was sitting on that chair an hour ago, and is now talking to Miss Duke in the garden.

"Yes, Innocent Smith has behaved here, as he has on hundreds of other occasions, upon a plain and perfectly blameless principle. It is odd and extravagant in the modern world, but not more than any other principle plainly applied in the modern world would be. His principle can be quite simply stated: he refuses to die while he is still alive. He seeks to remind himself by every electric shock to the intellect that he is still a man alive, walking on two legs about the world. For this reason he fires bullets at his best friends; for this reason he arranges ladders and collapsible chimneys to steal his own property; for this reason he goes plodding round a whole planet to get back to his own home. And for this reason he has been in the habit of taking the woman whom he loved with a permanent loyalty, and leaving her about (so to speak) at schools, boarding-houses, and places of business, so that he might recover her again and again with a raid and a romantic elopement. He seriously sought by a perpetual recapture of his bride to keep alive the sense of her perpetual value, and the perils that should be run for her sake.

"So far his motives are clear enough; but perhaps his convictions are not quite so clear. I think Innocent Smith has an idea at the bottom of all this. I am by no means sure that I believe it myself, but I am quite sure that it is worth a man's altering and defending.

"The idea that Smith is attacking is this. Living in an entangled civilization, we have come to think certain things wrong which are not wrong at all. We have come to think outbreak and exuberance, banging and barging, rotting and wrecking, wrong. In themselves they are not merely pardonable, they are unimpeachable. There is nothing wicked about firing off a pistol even at a friend; so long as you do not mean to hit him and know you won't. It is no more wrong than throwing a pebble at the sea—less; for you do occasionally hit the sea. There is nothing wrong in bashing down a chimney-pot and breaking through a roof, so long as you are not injuring the life or property of other men. It is no more wrong to choose to enter a house from the top, than to choose to open a packing-case from the bottom. There is nothing wicked about walking round the world and coming back to your own house; it is no more wicked than walking round the garden and coming back to your own house. And there is nothing wicked about picking up your wife here, there, and everywhere, if, forsaking all others, you keep only to her so long as you both shall live. It is as innocent as playing a game of hide-and-seek in the garden. You associate such acts with blackguardism by a mere snobbish association; as you think there is something vaguely vile about going (or being seen going) into a pawnbroker's or a public-house. You think there is something squalid and commonplace about such a connection. You are mistaken.

"This man's spiritual power has been precisely this: that he has distinguished between custom and creed. He has broken the conventions, but he has kept the commandments. It is as if a man were found gambling wildly in a gambling hell, and you found that he only played for trouser buttons. It is as if you found a man making a clandestine appointment with a lady at a Covent Garden ball, and then you found it was his grandmother. Everything is ugly and discreditable, except the facts. Everything is wrong about him, except that he has done no wrong.

"It will then be asked, 'Why does Innocent Smith continue far into his middle age a farcical existence, that exposes him to so many false charges?' To this I merely answer, that he does it because he really is happy, because he really is hilarious, because he really is a man and alive. He is so young, that climbing garden trees and playing silly practical jokes are still to him what they once were to us all. And if you ask me yet again why he alone among men should be fed with such inexhaustible follies, I have a very simple answer to that, though it is one that will not be approved.

"There is but one answer, and I am sorry if you don't like it. If Innocent is happy it is because he is innocent. If he can defy the conventions it is just because he can keep the commandments. It is just because he does not want to kill, but to excite to life that a pistol is still as exciting to him as it is to a schoolboy. It is just because he does not want to steal, because he does not covet his neighbour's goods, that he has captured the trick (oh, how we all long for it!), the trick of coveting his own goods. It is just because he does not want to commit adultery that he achieves the romance of sex; it is just because he loves one wife that he has a hundred honeymoons. If he had really murdered a man, if he had really deserted a woman, he would not be able to feel that a pistol or a love-letter was like a song. At least not a comic song.

u Do not imagine, please, that any such attitude is easy to me or appeals in any particular way to my sympathies. I am an Irishman, and a certain sorrow is in my bones, bred either of the persecutions of my creed, or of my creed itself. Speaking singly, I feel as if man was tied to tragedy, and there was no way out of the trap of old age and doubt. But if there is a way out, then, by Christ and St. Patrick, this is the way out. If one could keep as happy as a child or a dog, it would be by being as innocent as a child, or as sinless as a dog. Barely and brutally to be good, that may be the road, and he may have found it. Well, well, well, I see a look of scepticism on the face of my old friend Moses. Mr. Gould does not believe that being perfectly good in all respects would make a man hilarious."

"No," said Gould with an unusual and convincing gravity; "I do not believe that being perfectly good in all respects would make a man hilarious."

"Well," said Michael quietly, "will you tell me one thing? Which of us has ever tried it?"

A silence ensued, rather like the silence of some long geological epoch which awaits the emergence of some unexpected type; for there rose at last in the stillness a massive figure that the other men had almost completely forgotten.

"Well, gentlemen," said Dr. Warner cheerfully, "I've been pretty well entertained with all this pointless and incompetent tomfoolery for a couple of days; but it seems to be wearing rather thin, and I'm engaged for a city dinner. Among the hundred flowers of futility on both sides, I was unable to detect any sort of reason why a lunatic should be allowed to shoot me in the back garden."

He had settled his silk hat on his head and gone out sailing placidly to the garden gate, while the almost wailing voice of Pym still followed him • "But really the bullet missed you by several feet." And another voice added: "The bullet missed him by several years."

There was a long and mainly unmeaning silence, and then Moon said suddenly, "we have been sitting with a ghost. Dr. Herbert Warner died years ago."

## CHAPTER V
## HOW THE GREAT WIND WENT FROM BEACON HOUSE

MARY was walking between Diana and Rosamund slowly up and down the garden; they were silent, and the sun had set. Such spaces of daylight as remained open in the west were of a warm-tinted white, which can be compared to nothing but a cream cheese; and the lines of plumy cloud that ran across them had a soft but vivid violet bloom, like a violet smoke. All the rest of the scene swept and faded away into a dove-like gray, and seemed to melt and mount into Mary's dark-gray figure until she seemed clothed with the garden and the skies. There was something in these last quiet colours that gave her a setting and a supremacy; and the twilight which concealed Diana's statelier figure and Rosamund's braver array exhibited and emphasized her, leaving her the lady of the garden, and alone.

When they spoke at last, it was evident that a conversation long fallen silent was being suddenly revived.

"But where is your husband taking you?" asked Diana in her practical voice.

"To an aunt," said Mary; "that's just the joke. There really is an aunt, and we left the children with her when I arranged to be turned out of the other boarding-house down the road. We never take more than a week of this kind of holiday, but sometimes we take two of them together."

"Does the aunt mind much?" asked Rosamund innocently. "Of course, I dare say it's very narrow-minded and—what's that other word, you know, what Goliath was?—but I've known many aunts who would think it—well, silly."

"Silly?" cried Mary with great heartiness. "Oh, my Sunday hat! I should think it was silly! But what do you expect? He really is a good man, and it might have been snakes or something."

"Snakes?" inquired Rosamund, with a slightly puzzled interest.

"Uncle Harry kept snakes, and said they

loved him," replied Mary with perfect simplicity. "Auntie let him have them in his pockets, but not in the bedroom."

"And you—" began Diana, knitting her dark brows a little.

u Oh, I do as auntie did," said Mary; "as long as we're not away from the children more than a fortnight together, I play the game. He calls me 'Manalive,' and you must write it all in one word, or he's quite flustered."

"But if men want things like that—" began Diana.

"Oh, what's the good of talking about men," cried Mary impatiently; "why, one might as well be a lady novelist, or some horrid thing. There aren't any men. There are no such people. There's a man; and whoever he is he's quite different."

"So there's no safety," said Diana, in a low voice.

"Oh, I don't know," answered Mary lightly enough; "there's only two things generally true of them. At certain curious times they're just fitted to take care of us, and they're never fit to take care of themselves."

"There is a gale getting up," said Rosamund suddenly. "Look at those trees over there, a long way off, and the clouds going quicker."

"I know what you're thinking about," said Mary; "and don't you be silly fools. Don't you listen to the lady novelists. You go down the king's highway for God's truth; it is God's. Yes, my dear Michael will often be extremely untidy. Arthur Inglewood will be worse— he'll be tidy. But what else are all the trees and clouds for, you silly kittens?"

"The clouds and trees are all waving about," said Rosamund. "There is a storm coming, and it makes me feel quite excited, somehow. Michael is really rather like a storm; he frightens me and makes me happy."

"Don't you be frightened," said Mary. "All over, these men have one advantage: they are the sort that go out."

A sudden thrust of wind through the trees drifted the dying leaves along the path, and they could hear the far-off trees roaring faintly.

"I mean," said Mary, "they are the kind that look outwards and get interested in the world. It doesn't matter a bit whether it's arguing, or bicycling, or breaking down the ends of the earth as poor old Innocent does. Stick to the man who looks out of the window and tries to understand the world. Keep clear of the man who looks in at the window and tries to understand you. When poor old Adam had gone out gardening (Arthur will go out gardening) the other sort came along and wormed himself in, nasty old snake."

"You agree with your aunt," said Rosamund smiling; "no snakes in the bedroom."

"I didn't agree with my aunt very much," replied Mary simply, "but I think she was right to let Uncle Harry collect dragons and griffins, so long as it got him out of the house."

Almost at the same moment lights sprang up inside the darkened house, turning the two glass doors into the garden into gates of beaten gold. The golden gates were burst open, and the enormous Smith, who had sat like a clumsy statue for as many hours, came flying and turning cart-wheels down the lawn and shouting: "Acquitted! acquitted!" Echoing the cry, Michael scampered across to Rosamund and wildly swung her into a few steps of what was supposed to be a waltz. But the company knew Innocent and Michael by this time and their extravagances were wildly taken for granted; it was far more extraordinary that Arthur Inglewood walked straight up to Diana and kissed her as if it had been his sister's birthday. Even Dr. Pym, though he refrained from dancing, looked on with real benevolence; for indeed the whole of the absurd revelation had disturbed him less than the others; he half-supposed that such irresponsible tribunals and insane discussions were part of the mediaeval mummeries of the Old Land.

While the tempest tore the sky as with trumpets, window after window was lighted up in the house within; and before the company, broken with laughter and the buffeting of the wind, had groped their way to the house again, they saw that the great apish figure of Innocent Smith had clambered out of his own attic window, and roaring again and again, "Beacon House!" whirl round his head a huge log or trunk from the wood fire below of which the river of crimson flame and purple smoke drove out on the deafening air.

He was evident enough to have been seen from three counties; but when the wind died down, and the party at the top of their evening's merriment looked again for Mary and for him, they were not to be found.

THE END

Copyright, 1912, by
JOHN LANE COMPANY

Printed in the USA
CPSIA information can be obtained
at www.ICGtesting.com
CBHW081120081224
18657CB00026B/596